THE LIGHTS OF YSTRAC'S WOOD

A TALE OF THE SEVEN GODS

THE LIGHTS OF YSTRAC'S WOOD

A Tale of the Seven Gods

ALEXANDRA ROWLAND

CONTENTS

CHAPTER ONE

I N THE MIDDLE OF the isle of Avaris, there was a great and ancient greenwood that spanned miles and miles. A few settlements were scattered through it, but only around the outer part where people could make their living as woodsmen or hunters or farmers, coppicing the forest in a neverending negotiation between the wilderness and civilization.

In the center of the forest, the very heart of it, was a place where no one lived at all—a place that very few people could say that they had even *walked* through. They called it the godwood, the sacred wood of Ystrac—but then, all woods belonged to Ystrac in one way or another. He was the god of wilderness, the hunt, the keeper of the deer and the fox, the god of fear—and from his godwood emanated a creeping wilderness-panic. That sudden empathy with what it felt like to be *prey* was too strong for most people to tolerate for even an hour, and it took much longer than that to pass through the most fearsome part of the forest.

There was one road, just one, as straight as possible. It took most of a day's journey to pass from one end to the other, so long as a traveler did not stop or linger, and the beginning and end of it were marked, unnecessarily, with standing stones—unnecessary because that was where the lanterns of the wood began, where the panic really began to set in.

But the road was important—there was no other way to get through the wood, not without a traveler going weeks out of their way. On each side of the wood, and all around it, there were people, and cities, and trade: On one side, farmland, small towns and villages; on the other, the great capital of Brassing-on-Abona, the site of that ancient battle where the favored ones of the gods had gathered with their tribes and armies and had prayed to the gods for assistance and intervention to drive the invaders from their shores. Ystrac had a wood there, too, on the site where his favored one and the tribe she belonged to had camped before the battle, and afterwards where they had planted trees and allowed the wilderness to creep in and take hold. The other gods had henges, of course—but then, the other gods were civilized.

Aneth had never been to Brassing-on-Abona. She had grown up in the greenwood, Ystrac's Wood—the part that people lived in. Her father had been a woodsman; her mother, a weaver.

Aneth's mother had tried to teach her to weave, but the orderliness, the rhythm, the *civilized-ness* of the craft had driven Aneth to frustration. She had always been much closer to her father's trade; as a child, she had gone with him into the woods so he could assess the health of the trees, mark which ones needed to be thinned out to make room for others to grow strong and tall. He taught her how to hunt, how to walk silently, how to use a bow or slingshot or cunning traps, how to field-dress her kill. The first night they had ever camped out in the woods, Aneth had lain awake and looked at the trees arching up to scrape the starry sky above, and had thrilled with wilderness-fear. In that moment, and in all moments since, she had thought that it was preferable, vastly, to sleeping beneath a thatch and rafters and blankets on a soft bed.

By the time she was a young woman, it had long since become clear to everyone—her father, her mother, the others in her village, herself—that she was one of Ystrac's own. Whether she was one of his favored ones, that was more uncertain. Favor was only granted once in a generation, if that, and it was not always obvious enough to tell, especially for a god such as Ystrac. There were gradations of favor, they said—but that too sounded to Aneth like civilized nonsense. What did she care for gradations or classifications or whether or not she could be sorted into a convenient box? The wilds cared nothing for such things, and so neither did Aneth.

Dedicates of Ystrac rarely had fixed abode, and if they did, they were even more rarely to be found there. Aneth had a bed in the house which had once belonged to her parents, which now belonged to her brother and his wife. She slept there through the bitterest weeks of winter, and then she went back out into the woods.

Her apprenticeship had been to many masters, and had taken many years—whenever someone who had dedicated themself to Ystrac came through the village, she had spent a day or two with them, talking about the woods and the hunt, the legends of Ystrac, tales of his favored ones from times long past, and what he might require of those who felt kinship with him.

So Aneth walked the woods, and learned about fear, and the ways of the forest, and what it was like to live on the boundary between the safe, settled lands and the wilderness, where all that mattered was how sharp your eyes were, how keen your ears, how swift your feet, how hungry your belly.

It was not a comfortable life, but she thought she would have been bored with that—and there was a difference between *comfortable* and *comfort*. Ystrac's priests were still human, after all, as complex as any others, and they—including Aneth—enjoyed pleasant or pleasurable things:

A hot meal, a warm fireside, beautiful things. It was just (or so Aneth had found, from years of talking to others aligned with Ystrac, years of having a great deal of quiet time with her own thoughts) that they had different ideas from most people about what was beautiful. Her brother thought jewels were beautiful, and that his wife was beautiful, and that it was therefore twice as beautiful if his wife was wearing a pretty cloak-pin made of bright-polished copper and pebbles of colored glass.

Aneth, on the other hand, thought the moment when the woods fell silent and the hairs raised on her arms was beautiful. She thought a carpet of bluebells in spring was beautiful, or sunrise over the forest viewed from a perch on a craggy hill, or the feeling of being *utterly* alone, or the sound of her voice as she sang along with the birds, or the taste of hot pine-needle tea drunk from her little clay cup underneath a rocky overhang as the rain fell and her campfire crackled.

Those were the most beautiful things she could imagine.

So she walked the forest, and she gave what service she could to Ystrac, and she was happy.

One of the necessary works that the kin of Ystrac saw to was guiding travelers along the road through that deepest part of the forest, offering them protection and companionship when the fear of the woods threatened to madden their minds and addle their senses.

The only thing that kept the wilderness-panic from growing too powerful and fearsome to resist were the lanterns. The road itself was not remarkable—no magic had been laid upon it, so far as Aneth knew—but the lanterns...

Aneth had walked the Highway herself many times, and sometimes her curiosity had overtaken her and driven her to peep inside the lanterns. None of them had a reservoir for oil, nor wood for kindling. Despite this, the flames within burned steady and bright, only flickering slightly once in a long while. The only thing she knew about the lanterns was that from time to time, one of the priests of Talesyn—the god of fire, amongst other things—would come out to the woods to walk the road and see to them.

The lanterns were all different, though most were made of some kind of brownish-gold metal (copper or bronze or brass, she wasn't sure) and glass. Some were nicer than others—the metal wrought in fancy designs, or decorate with something Aneth thought that her brother might call piercework or filigree. The glass was all clear—not like the colored glass pebbles from her sister-in-law's pretty cloakpin—but not always perfect. Some of the panes were streaked with tiny bubbles which glittered and caught the light of the steady flame within, especially in the purple light of gloaming. Some had a slightly wobbly surface, and when Aneth looked through them, it was like looking through rippling water to the streambed beneath. Some were hung from the branches that overhung the path, some from poles set into the ground, about the height of a rider on horseback. Some were balanced on top of rocks, or hung from mounting arms bolted into the living trees. Aneth had wondered once if Ystrac might take offense to such a thing, and then had laughed under her breath for the rest of the day at the idea that someone might think that Ystrac—or the forest—would pay the slightest heed to such a thing. The trees were ancient; the forest was ancient; Ystrac had already been ancient when the forest was no more than a handful of seedlings. What did they care for a couple bolts in the side of a single tree? The tree itself didn't care—it went on growing, sprouting leaves and seeds, reaching deep into the earth and high into the sky.

Aneth was curious about the lanterns and what they were for, but she knew only what anyone knew—that they helped travelers, that they kept the road safe, that they held back the wilderness-panic just enough to allow folk to pass along the road without fleeing in terror like spooked deer.

It was one day in late spring—as fine a day as ever had been—when Aneth stepped out of the forest onto gravel and cobbles and found that her feet had carried her to the standing stone at one end of the road through Ystrac's Wood.

Calling it an *end* was kind of a funny thing, as it was quite definitely a middle of the road when you looked at it, but that was what people said. It was like it became, temporarily, a different road entirely as it ran through the godwood.

As she always did when she came to this part of the forest, she made her way up to the standing stone to leave offerings to Ystrac. There were always a number of offerings, laid in the grass at its foot, wrapped in leaves or folded handkerchiefs. There were trees nearby with ribbons tied to their branches, too. Aneth had a full pack of rations, having passed through a village the day before—in addition to all the rest, Ystrac was also the god of wanderers and travellers, and so people were often willing to curry favor with him by offering assistance to his kin and anyone that looked like they might be his kin. Hermits who lived in the forest, beggars and wanderers... Put enough twigs in your hair and rub dirt on your face and most anyone you asked would give you a loaf or a few pieces of jerky or waybread. Most of the time, Aneth didn't even have to ask. Ystrac was not a popular god, not a god most people found relatable or friendly—but still one who had useful blessings to bestow.

Well, and he was generally feared, especially by those in the countryside who had brushed up against true wilderness before.

Aneth was thinking that it was just about lunchtime (and that splitting half a piece of waybread with Ystrac would probably do nicely as an offering) when she saw, sitting at the bottom of the stone, a man.

Quite the most absurd-looking man she had ever seen in her life, and not only for the distinctly hangdog expression on his face.

He had a hat with far too many feathers on it, the kind with a pointed front and a turned-up brim in the back. He had a lute or something across his lap, though he was not playing it. He had a coat the color of red grapes, and glittering things hanging from his ears, and more glittery things on his wrists, and the oddest boots Aneth had ever seen.

He looked up, just as she came onto the road, and jumped violently.

He *jangled.* This was confounding enough that Aneth stopped in her tracks, staring at him in bewilderment.

A moment later, his expression cleared, then lit with pleasure. "Hail, as they say, and well-met! Dare I to hope that you are one of the kin of Ystrac?"

"Yes," said Aneth, coming forward. "I am." She studied him again as she slid her bag off her shoulder and dug out a piece of waybread, tossing it onto the grass before the great grey standing stone, its face carved shallowly with an depiction of Ystrac which may well have been older than many of the trees—the crude representation of the figure was tall, with broad-shoulders, antlers sprouting from his head, a cloak of leaves, a club in one hand and a spear in the other. Besides the cloak of oak leaves, he was naked, and whichever ancient stone carver had made this had gone to some trouble to detail the swirls of thick hair on his chest and the vigor of his erection. Aneth regarded the carving fondly for a moment. Did she like this one better than the one at the other end of the road? It was hard to say—she liked whichever one she was standing in front of, probably.

Hallo, Ystrac. Show me the path when there is no path, and let my feet be silent. Slow the hare and hart that my hunt might be fruitful, and keep the wolf and elk and boar and bear upwind, that I may pass without trouble. Enjoy your bread. You know where to find me if there is service I can do you.

She turned back to the strange man. He was probably one service that needed doing. "Are you going to the other end?"

"Yes," he said, seeming much relieved. He jangled to his feet—Aneth saw that his coat was rather... swoopy. It was shaped like a jerkin at the top, but then the bottom flared out to this... skirt-like thing, which was (astonishingly) also extremely glittery and jangly. The bottom hem had little gold-colored discs hanging from it which chimed gently against each other as he moved. His boots, she now saw, were thigh-high, lacing up the sides, made of what seemed to be quite thin and supple leather, as they hugged his feet snugly—custom made, then, just for him, not made to fit one of the cobbler's standard lasts. The leather was several shades darker than his coat, and around one ankle (*over* the leather of the boot, absurdly and bewilderingly), he wore another jangly piece of jewelry. The heels of the boots were carved wood, a couple inches high, which was what Aneth had originally thought so odd-looking about them, and they were painted in some kind of shiny gold stuff.

"Do you like them?" he said, turning his feet this way and that.

"What?"

"You were looking at my boots. Do you like them? They're new."

Aneth looked down at them again. "Personally, I would be worried about spoiling them on the road," she said, carefully polite. "They look... easily scuffed. And not very comfortable for walking."

"Oh, they're not," he said immediately. "Nothing close to it. That's why I was sitting down for a bit, my feet are killing me. But that's the price of beauty," he added with a noble sigh. "I thought that if I had to go down the lantern path all by myself on my lonesome and be gobbled up by ferocious beasts or monsters, or driven mad until I run into the woods in terror and get lost and wander around for weeks until I starve to death, only for my body to be found a mere dozen feet away from the road, then I would like the corpse to be, first, easily distinguishable as mine, and second, a good looking one. Or at least well-dressed, since corpses probably don't look that good after lying around on the ground for a while."

He said all this with extraordinary solemnity. "Which is why I have come all the way out to Ystrac's Wood in my nicest clothes. And my new boots," he said, pointing one foot out before him in illustration, whereupon he was distracted for a moment with the pleasure of looking at it himself, gazing down with an expression of great satisfaction as he turned his foot again from one side to another, rather elegantly, like a dancer.

"I see," said Aneth, unsure how to respond except with equal solemnity. "That's very clever of you."

"Thank you," he said, nodding. It made the jewelry-thing dangling from his ears swing and dance, glittering in the light and tinkling softly. "But now I've been fortunate enough to run into one of Ystrac's kin, and perhaps my fate is not yet sealed! May I beg the traditional boon of you? Will you accompany me to the other end of this road, and protect me from Ystrac's mischief so that I might leave this place with life and boots intact? They're new boots, you see, did I mention that? Oh, I did, didn't I."

Aneth was sure it would be impolite to laugh at him, and so she didn't. "Yes, I will accompany you."

"Only it will take quite a long time, I think," he said with a little grimace. His lips were a bit shiny, as if he'd rubbed them with the beeswax balm that folks in Aneth's village used to protect their lips from chapping in the winter wind. Except it was spring.

"Your boots," she said with a sage nod. "How often do you need to sit and rest?"

"Oh, once or twice an hour."

"Ystrac's eyes."

"Yes, I know. But no, it's not that—or not just that. It's that I have to—oh, forgive me, I haven't even introduced myself." He swept off his hat and bowed to her—no one had ever done that to her before and she wasn't entirely sure how to feel about it. He'd done it in a fancy way too, with one pointed foot extended slightly and turned out. Everything on him jangled or tinkled or chimed, or at minimum glittered in the sunshine. "My name is Corentin, and just as you are kin of Ystrac, so too am I kin of Talesyn Silverthroat, Lord of Poets, the Songspinner—or, as is more relevant at this precise moment, the Lord of Flame."

"Ah," said Aneth, still utterly solemn. "That explains a lot."

Corentin burst out laughing. "Madam, are you suggesting I am in any way a walking cliche of my type?"

"Oh, I don't know about that," said Aneth, who didn't know what a cliche was, or whether it was good or not for one to be walking. "You're here for the lanterns, then, I take it?"

"Why else would a priest of Clevertongue come all the way out to the middle of the forest, and all on his lonesome?"

"And in his new boots."

"Yes indeed!"

Aneth's mouth quirked—her amusement was quickly exceeding her ability to keep a completely straight face. She glanced down at his boots again. They looked nice enough—they certainly made his legs look long and lithe, like a deer's. The ankle jewelry was perhaps a bit of overkill. "I take it as well that you're from the city?"

"Brassing-on-Abona, yes. I can't say that I much care for the country and all this fresh air—no offense intended, my lord," he said, with another elegant bow to the standing stone. To Aneth, he added with a grin, "I suppose that's why you're his and I'm not."

"Suppose so," she agreed. Ystrac wouldn't care about Corentin's opinion of the fresh air any more than he cared about a lantern bolted to a tree. "Long way to come just for the lanterns. We've got Talesyn priests out here too. Usually they're the ones to handle it. Since they're familiar with the terrain, you know."

"I do know it," Corentin said affably. "And if I had my choice, I'd be back in the city right now."

"Lost a wager, eh?"

"That's one way of looking at it." He looked her right in the eye and smiled, and something low in her stomach swooped and fluttered, and she understood suddenly why Talesyn and his priests had the reputation they did—he was impossible to look away from. Magnetic, almost. It wasn't quite desire—she knew plenty of desire, and this was like it, but not precisely so. She was holding her breath, she noticed, waiting for the next thing he said. There was the feeling of a resonance in the air, a tension drawing out, like the moment before an archer loosed their bow and hit their target dead-on. Whatever Corentin said next was going to be absolute truth, she knew. Truth like in the stories. Truth like the strength of an ancient oak in the center of a wood.

Corentin had a dancing light in his eyes like he knew it too. His smile was small, private—and no less powerful for all that. In a voice no different than what he had been using thus far, and yet entirely different, he said: "During the last gathering of my colleagues for the ritual mysteries,

I boasted before the entire assembled body of them that I bore the divine mark of Lord Talesyn's favor. I have come to... ah, put my money where my mouth is, shall we say."

It took Aneth a moment to collect herself.

"Was it just a boast?"

"Who's to say?" he said with an elegant little shrug of one shoulder. "I feel instinctively that Clevertongue wouldn't give his favor to someone unless they were audacious and brazen enough to claim it, so." His smile broadened. "It is said that my lord rewards boldness."

"As does mine," Aneth admitted, glancing up again at the carving of Ystrac. "I don't think he would give his favor to someone who was cowardly or meek."

"Leave that to the favored of Angarat and Mategat," Corentin said with a nod. "Ah, that sounded boorish, didn't it? Nothing against either of the good ladies, I celebrate their works and their blessings as much as anyone does. I only meant that they do not require the same sort of qualities in their favored ones that Lord Ystrac and Lord Talesyn do."

"Did the others... force you to come out here?"

"Not at all. I was asking for it, wasn't I?" he said lightly.

"Yes, a bit." He laughed. She shook her head and went on, "I meant, is this required in your mysteries? To prove you have Talesyn's favor? Or did you volunteer it? Or did they dare you?"

He put his head a little on one side, his earrings swinging and twinkling, the feathers on his hat bobbing. "You know, I'm not sure. I was a little drunk at the time, you see."

"I see," said Aneth, the amusement bubbling up again. She fought it down. "Well, do you have rations enough for the journey?" He stepped aside and pointed at a bag leaning against the base of the standing stone, which had been hidden by the sweep of his coat's skirts. He jangled and tinkled as he moved—his ankle jewelry, his dozens of bracelets, the twinkly metal things on the bottom of his coat. But the bag looked big enough to carry a week's worth of food, which should be more than enough. Within the godwood, it would be difficult enough for Aneth to supplement her own supply with the bounty of the forest—feeding two, one of whom was not kin of Ystrac, would have been a daunting prospect. "And have you made your gifts to the Lord of the Wilds?"

"I was putting it off, on account of being scared out of my wits," he said cheerfully, but dug in some inner pocket of his coat and produced a silver coin, which he made to throw in the grass before the stone.

"No," said Aneth, before he could. "Give him something better than that."

"I always leave money on his festival days," Corentin protested mildly, but tucked the coin away and dug around again. "He's never seemed to mind before."

"Have you ever left the city before?"

"Well, no. Hm, I'm not sure what else I have that would be appropriate. Ought I leave some of my food? I'd rather conserve it, and it seems a bit... casual and overfamiliar."

Aneth considered this. "Maybe so."

"I could sing him a song, do you think that would do?" He held his lute up by the neck.

Aneth regarded it dubiously. She wasn't sure that Ystrac cared much for song, except those of birds, or the work-songs people sang as they felled a tree or field-dressed the prize of their hunt. "Give him one of your feathers," she said decisively.

Corentin looked vaguely horrified by this, but pulled the hat off his head again and picked through the feathers with only a little show of moroseness. "Removing any one will spoil the effect of the whole, but I suppose it wouldn't be a worthy sacrifice if it didn't feel like it cost something to give." Aneth watched him, wondering if he would choose the smallest or the blandest. He did not—he chose a fine green-dyed pheasant feather which had been steam-shaped into a dramatic curl. He put the hat back on his head (Aneth noted ruefully that he was right; losing that one did rather spoil the effect) and held the feather up to the stone.

"Lord Ystrac, I do not begrudge you this, though I own it is a wrench to give it up. I received this as a gift once, on the occasion of the Earl of Westershore's wedding, when I sang him and his bride a song that brought both their families to tears and settled the feud that had been about to erupt over an offense the Earl made in error. In gratitude, he granted me this, a feather from the very hat he was wearing that day, and moreover told me the tale of the merry hunt on which he had won it and the once-in-a-lifetime shot that brought the bird down. I keep the tale, Lord of the Wilds, but I return the feather to you. I beseech you to be satisfied, and to allow us to pass through your wood in peace."

Aneth found herself deeply impressed and approving—all that charm and charisma the kin of Talesyn were reputed to have was good for something after all! What pretty manners, and what elegant grace. "Show us the path when there is no path, Great Hunter," she murmured. "And let our feet be silent."

There was no sound but the sound of the birdsong for several long moments, and the breeze rustling in the trees.

At last, Corentin turned to her with a businesslike nod. "Not much chance of silent feet, I'm afraid, even with Lord Ystrac's blessing. Do you know, I had never noticed how loud my clothes were? Not until I got out here on my own and it was just me and the birds."

"I wasn't going to say anything," Aneth said mildly, and he laughed again.

They crossed the border into the godwood. Aneth had walked this road many times before, but even she was not spared the sudden unsettling sense that the woods on either side of the road were no longer quite the woods she knew, that the birdsong was either too loud or not loud enough, that there might be something in the treeline watching them...

But she knew the woods and the wilds well enough to know that there was indeed usually something keeping an eye on her, but oftener than not it was out of wariness that she was the *predator* to run from, not the potential prey. She rolled her shoulders and her neck and breathed deep, opening herself to the fear, turning towards it in her mind to examine it with welcome and curiosity—which of course went a long way to making it vanish like mist under warm sunshine. Two or three breaths later, all that was left was a slight singing tension along her nerves, a thrilling sense of imminence, a sizzle of excitement to keep her on her toes. She never felt so alive as when she was in the godwood—except for the time she'd hunted boar or bear alone.

Corentin was worse off. He was pale, shuddering so hard that all his tinkly jewelry was jangling at once—even his lute seemed to be sounding softly. He had edged up to Aneth's side and unconsciously reached out to touch her sleeve, looking around at the forest like a little rabbit frozen in terror.

Aneth tucked his hand around her arm and said, "Let's go. You have to walk it off."

"I don't know that I can, madam," he said, his voice perfectly steady and conversational though he was trembling like a newborn fawn trying to find its feet.

She realized suddenly that she hadn't told him her name. "Aneth. Not madam."

"Aneth," he said faintly, his eyes still on the woods.

She tugged him a little by his grip on her elbow. "Come on, Corentin. Brazenness and—whatever that other thing was that you said Lord Talesyn appreciates."

"Audacity."

"That's the one."

It took a little more coaxing, but his absurd heeled boots made him unsteady on his feet, so he was easy enough to offbalance, and a couple stumbling little steps forward helped him find his momentum. The heels made him just an inch or two taller than her—if they'd both been bare-foot, they would have been the same height, or close to it.

He didn't let go of her arm even when his strides length-ened. The jangling—oh, he was very loud, wasn't he—be-came a rhythmic accompaniment to the sound of their shoes on the worn stones of the road. Hers thudded; his were distinctly clicky.

The first lantern was one perhaps even more ancient than the standing stone. It was waist-high, a simple rough column of stone with hollows cut in near the top, little tunnels just big enough to put a hand through. The flame within burned steadily, even without any glass to protect it, and in all the times that Aneth had walked the path, she had never seen it flickering or burning low.

Corentin made a desperate sound of relief when they came near it and dropped her arm, falling to his knees by the lantern and... well, hugging it, Aneth supposed that was. Clinging to it, maybe, like it was the only thing be-sides her arm that felt safe in these woods.

"Clevertongue, my lord, grant me boldness. Oh, I hate this. This is so much worse than stage fright."

Aneth wasn't sure whether he was talking to her or to Lord Talesyn. "Well, people watching you on stage proba-bly aren't interested in eating you."

He sat back on his heels, his hands on his thighs, and took a few steadying breaths. "Boldness," he said, now sounding as if he were speaking to himself in resolution.

"Boldness and brazenness," Aneth agreed. "You can do this."

"You're so kind to me," he quavered, as if he were thinking of crying. "I didn't expect—well." He gave a mighty sniffle and shook himself. "I thought one of Ystrac's kin would be… less kind. That they might laugh at me, or sneer. At least I knew if I ran into one of you that I could ask for help and that I wouldn't be denied." He slipped the strap of his bag off his shoulder and reached into one of the side pockets, pulling out a wodge of paper. "But help isn't always given in kindness. It would have been unpleasant to do all this with my guide and protector laughing at me the whole way. I thought it would be a humiliating experience." He used the wodge of paper to gesture at all his clothes and jewelry. "Hence the battle armor, you know."

"I thought it was so your dead body could be identified."

"That as well, yes."

He flicked through the wodge and selected a sheet, replacing the rest in his bag. He rolled the sheet up neatly and pushed it into the hollow of the lamp where the flame burned. It did not change in intensity or steadiness, but Aneth noticed the tension of her nerves easing slightly—like a stoked fire blazed hotter to push the cold back, the lantern was doing something to push the wilderness-fear back. She had not noticed that in the other times when she had passed along the road, but she had never had kin of Talesyn with her.

"Songspinner, Lord of Flame, strengthen my voice," Corentin whispered, almost too quiet for her to hear. "I am bid by my fellows to walk the lantern path and bring your light and warmth to these dark places, for your gifts are those that keep the wolves from our hearts in the times when all else is lost." In a rather different voice, reaching out to clutch at the lantern again and leaning his forehead against it, he added plaintively, "The things I *do* for you, Clevertongue! Stage fright, of all things! Me! Stage fright!"

Aneth bit her lip to keep from chuckling at him.

After a moment, he sighed, and got to his feet, brushing the dust from his coat and his boots. "Oh, look at that, I've scuffed them a bit already." He rubbed sadly at the marks on the knees and toes of his boots, licked his thumb, and rubbed them again.

"You fell to your knees very dramatically," Aneth said, finding to her slight surprise and amusement that all this silliness of Corentin's was rather endearing. "What did you expect?"

"Oh, I don't know. I was overcome. I didn't expect anything." He picked up his bag, hung its strap from his shoulder, and took her arm again. "Onwards."

"You don't want to rest? How are your feet?"

"Killing me, thank you for asking."

They got about a third of the way through Ystrac's wood by sunset. Corentin attended to each of the lanterns the same, though he didn't throw himself to his knees for the others. He began singing as the afternoon faded into evening, his hand tightening on Aneth's arm, and he only stopped to fuel the fires of each lantern with paper and prayer or whatever it was he was doing.

Her own Ystrac required very few rituals, even from his kin. There were offerings the villagers made to the forest, and the ritual sharing of the hunt between the hunters and the Hunter. But by and large, Ystrac cared more for the *living* of his way than he did for the *performance* of it.

Aneth reflected with amusement that it only made sense that the Lord of Poets and Players would appreciate a little performance.

They made camp—or what passed for it—by what Aneth remembered as the largest and most significant lantern for several more hours' walk. It was a great glass orb hung from a branch that arched over the path, an orb large enough that Aneth could have sat in it comfortably with her legs crossed tailor-style. Over the years or decades, the branch had sagged under the weight, and now the decorative metal finial on the bottom of the orb was resting directly on the ground. It had a fine fire in it, but it gave off no warmth but the easing of fear.

Aneth built a proper fire on the road, using what twigs she could gather without stepping off the path. One of the twigs, fortuitously, turned out to be the very end of a huge dry branch that had been covered up with overgrown grasses and shrubs. Aneth pulled it out of the underbrush with a grin and set to breaking it into campfire-sized chunks. The Lord of the Wilds was in a tenderhearted mood today, apparently. She did not thank him, as the villagers did, for she had always felt that he cared as little for sweet words and ardent declarations as she did, but she resolved to make a particularly fine arrow to leave for him at the next stone or sacred place of his that she came across after they were out of his Wood. Ashwood for the shaft, and new iron for the head, and the best fletching she could find.

When they sat beside the campfire that evening with their backs against the orb, Corentin tucked close to her side, she discovered that he didn't have much food in his pack at all—the majority of it was taken up with a very well-padded, cloth-wrapped bundle. If he had been anyone else, she might have been impatient and exasperated with him. Instead, all she said was, "What's that?"

Corentin looked at the bundle, swallowed his bite of bread and cheese, and said, "A new lantern for the path."

"Oh. I didn't know that new ones get added."

"Only if you're as arrogant as I am," he said with a ghost of his earlier smile. The pressing fear had exhausted him, and he had refused to stop and rest his feet for more than the time it took to attend to each lantern.

"Audacious," she said, because he seemed like he needed to be reminded of himself. "Bold. Favored by Talesyn."

A slightly brighter smile, then, though somewhat rueful. "Just so."

When he had finished eating, he tuned his lute and played for a while, sometimes singing along, sometimes only playing. The songs were all quiet ones, calming, comforting.

Aneth listened in silence and wondered what precisely he was comforting himself about—the fear of Ystrac's Wood? The possibility that he might *not* be favored? That he might not be able to prove it if he was?

Drowsy, she asked, "What did you mean, about 'only if you're as arrogant as I am'?"

"You have to be quite favored indeed to call up the kind of fire burning in these," he said. "And I... Well. I never have before, but that doesn't mean anything. Someday I might."

"What kind of special fire is it, anyway?"

Corentin didn't reply for a long minute. When he spoke again, his voice was soft, gentle, wistful, yearning. "Awen."

She opened her eyes. Blinked at the campfire. Turned over her shoulder and looked into the flame burning in the orb behind her. "*Talesyn's* awen?" she asked dumbly.

"Who else's would it be?" He tilted his head back, looking up at the stars. "You see now why it takes one who is favored."

Awen—the fire of poetry, the light of inspiration, Talesyn's gift to his bards, his kin. Yes, she did see why.

"What have you been fueling it with?" she whispered.

"What we always fuel it with," Corentin replied with a shrug. "Poems I shall never write. Songs I shall never play. Visions of what the world could be. Ideas."

She had to sit in silence with this again. "But there are dozens more lanterns."

"Yes, I expect there are."

"And you're feeding them all your ideas for songs and things?"

"Yes," he said simply, as apparently unconcerned with this as he was with his aching feet, with the prospect of sacrificing a feather that reminded him of an important memory.

"What if you run out?'

He laughed as he had not laughed since they'd been at the standing stone. "There are always more ideas."

"But these you give up, they get consumed? As the campfire consumes the logs?"

"Such is the price of beauty, Aneth."

They didn't speak again that night. A few minutes later, he set aside his lute and curled up with his back to the campfire, facing the awen shining softly in the orb.

The next day, just before noon, they came upon a lantern which had fallen and shattered. Corentin was steadier by now—he had grown accustomed to the fear, though he still stuck close beside Aneth, his hand linked around her elbow.

He stopped and gazed at the lantern for a time. "Ah."

"I've never heard of one breaking before," Aneth said, unsettled. "Are they supposed to do that?"

"That's why the favored ones have to replace them sometimes."

He let go of her arm, which he had not done except in the presence of one of the lit lanterns—the flames of awen—and crouched by the fallen lantern. He brushed his fingers across the shards of glass, the pieces of twisted metal, and then he pulled his pack off his shoulder and set about unwrapping the bundle within. His hands were trembling. The fear pressed on them both. Even Aneth was exhausted with it. It wasn't good for the body to live in a heightened state like this for too long. It sharpened all the senses at first, but too much of it could break a person, leave them scarred long after they left this place.

Corentin withdrew a beautiful lantern—of course it was beautiful, it was his—and held it up. It was perhaps as big as their two heads together, with decorative metalwork above and below, the glass caged by strips of metal. There was a great ring on the top, and this Corentin caught on the hook of the previous lantern's support pole.

"How did you know that it would have to be this kind of lantern?" she asked.

"We'd heard word from one of the other priests of Talesyn who came through that this one was looking like it was about to go." He cast her a faint smile over his shoulder. "No one's inspiration is infinite."

"Whose was this? Do you know?"

"Elouan. He died two hundred years ago. He wrote the *Song of Summer,* I'm sure you know it."

"The one that's sung on Talesyn's feast day?"

"The very same."

It was strange to think that a song so familiar as to be commonplace had once been written by a *person.* Such a thing had never occurred to her before. With songs like that, it seemed like everyone was just *born* knowing them. She couldn't remember ever learning the *Song of Summer.*

She couldn't remember ever messing up the words when she headed home for Talesyn's feast day and went with her brother and his wife to lay a few offerings and light candles at Talesyn's shrine.

Corentin was holding his hanging lantern between his hands. She stepped closer and nudged her shoulder against his, to be a bastion against the fear pressing in from the forest around them. They must have been near the very center. She said nothing.

"Lord of Song," Corentin said aloud. "Yours was the first gift given to mortals, and all others follow from it. Before anything in this world can exist, before it can be done or made, before a song can be sung or a word can be spoken, before a wish can flower and fruit—before all else, first it must be thought of. Yours is the light that all thought follows, that all craft and art follows, that all human creation and accomplishment follows. I have come to walk the lantern path, Lord of Flame. Alight it."

The lantern between Corentin's hands stayed empty.

He pulled one of his little papers from his pocket—one of his ideas or poems or songs—and pushed it inside through a gap at the bottom of one of the panes of glass. "Come on, Silverthroat," he crooned. "Come on, you know you want to."

"That's more how you'd manage the Lord of Temptation, isn't it?" Aneth murmured. What strange things it must do to a person, to be fond of a god who could be bargained with.

"Probably, yes." Corentin stepped back, his fingers lingering on the glass for a moment. His expression was resolute, proud, determined. He pulled his lute on its strap around to his front. "This might take a while."

"I don't have anywhere to be."

She sat on the ground near the lantern, just on a comfortable tussock of grass, and she watched Corentin petition his lord.

He was magnificent. As magnificent as a carpet of bluebells unexpectedly discovered deep in the forest. As magnificent as a warm summer night with the stars above and a meadow full of twinkling fireflies. He sang, his voice strong and steady and sure, his fingers deft and nimble on the strings. He sang the *Song of Summer,* and "The Two Rings" (which Aneth had thought was only a silly children's song, but this version had a lot more verses and a much less gibberish chorus), and one about the Battle of the Bridge. There were a lot of others too, ones Aneth knew and ones she didn't; ones she didn't care for at all and ones that brought her to tears...

Talesyn ruled the time of day when the sun was highest in the sky; Corentin sang for the entirety of Talesyn's hours, and all through Brassu's after that, until the westering sun had slipped undeniably into the golden hours of Ystrac.

"Do you have enough food for tomorrow?" Aneth asked, when Corentin fell silent.

"Yes. If I can stand to be a little hungry," he said, voice rasping. She handed him her waterskin. He drank.

"If we start from here in the early morning, we can be out of the godwood by this time tomorrow and in the next village by midday the next." She stood, brushed the grass off her trousers, and looked into the forest. Fear welled up through her mind. She patted it gently. "I'll go refill our waterskins and see if I can find anything more to eat."

Corentin squeaked. "What! You're not going off into the woods!"

"I am."

He danced from foot to foot a little, wide eyed, jangling from his ears to his ankles, his feathers bobbling. "You'll be lost."

"Maybe. It's Ystrac's Wood, it's up to him."

"You'll be killed."

"Not if I can help it," she said, amused.

"You're stepping off the road, and the thing everyone always says is *not to step off the road in Ystrac's Wood.*"

It *was* practically a whatsits, a proverb. But... "That's not what Ystrac's kin say."

"The fear will drive me mad," he blurted.

"There's no reason to be afraid of fear," she said, stepping forward to take the waterskin from him. "It can't hurt you unless you let it."

"Oh, now who's a walking cliche!"

Impulsively, she kissed his cheek. He looked at her in astonishment, and she said, feigning the tenderness of a lover, "I don't know what a cliche is, Corentin."

He spluttered with laughter; she grinned and stepped back, turning towards the forest.

"Wait," he said, grabbing her arm. "Wait—what is it that Ystrac's kin say, if they don't say to stay on the road in the godwood?" He lowered his voice and added in a whisper, "Say something good, because I'm going to write a song about this later and everyone will expect you to say something really marvelous at this bit." Then, in his normal voice again—though his hands trembled on her arm: "What is it that the kin of Ystrac say, Brave Aneth?"

What a preposterous person he was, Aneth thought to herself fondly. Aloud—dare she say, dramatically—she said: "Show me the path where there is no path, and let my feet be silent."

This apparently struck Corentin so strongly that his grip on her arm went lax and she was able to slip free. "Oh, good," he whispered, gazing at her with deep admiration shining in his eyes. "Oh, very good."

"Was it?" she whispered back, half laughing as she stepped slowly backwards and away from him. "Will it do for your poem?"

"Oh, yes. Oh, marvelously."

And with that, she stepped off the road and into Ystrac's Wood.

Chapter Two

Aneth, Corentin's marvelous new acquaintance, stepped off the road. Corentin's knees were weak with fear, his heart tripping and stuttering in his chest at every unexpected sound, and as his guide and protector vanished into the trees, the rising haze of terror so his mind so addled that he felt like he could barely think, even as it brought the world into extraordinary focus—both foggy and razor-sharp.

That last was the worst part. It was like being drunk—it was like being *drugged*—and Corentin had never cared for either. He required his mind, his focus, his wit. He did not *like* to be impaired.

The fear was a severe impairment, and ooh, he did not like it *at all*.

It did not care. It pressed on him from every side, made his legs and hands shake and all his jewelry jingle, made his lungs gasp and pant for air, made his eyes dart around, looking for the danger behind every tree.

He had told Aneth and Lord Talesyn that it was like the worst stage fright he'd ever had, times a thousand, but that wasn't quite true. Stage fright *went away* after a bit—these days there was only the adrenaline-swoop of his stomach whenever he was about to step in front of an audience, but even in his early days, when he'd been new to it, stage-fright had only ever lasted five or six minutes, and then he'd settled into what he was doing, got the pace of things, relaxed as his little twitchy rabbit brain realized that no one was going to laugh at him or throw vegetables or boo him off the stage.

This fear, the wilderness fear, *did not abate.* It was terrifying—and exhausting. He kept thinking that he ought to be getting bored of it—he never felt stage fright when he was bored by his material, he wasn't sure that anyone could be bored and afraid at the same time—but the wilderness fear was a different kind of fear entirely.

It was the fear of the dark and the things in the dark; it was the wolves at the door and the specter of the unknown, the sudden and pressing sense that he was very, very small and the world was very, very big.

Another shudder ran through him, setting off another shimmering sound from all his jewelry and a low sound from his lute. He felt rather sick with fear, but being sick wouldn't do him any good.

Aneth barely seemed to feel the fear at all. He had no earthly idea how she managed it. She was one of the plainest people he had ever met—plain brown hair, plain sun-browned skin, plain eyes of some indeterminate color between grey and green and mud. Plain clothes—*very* plain clothes. Plain height and build—though admittedly on the strong and hale side of plain. But the more he watched her, the more he'd gotten the impression that it wasn't "plain" which was the right word... There *was no word* for what she was. She was quite literally indescribable—he had been thinking all day of how he might go about singing her praises in a song, and all adjectives escaped him. Quite a lot of nouns, too. You couldn't use the word "tresses" about Aneth's hair, for example. It wouldn't have fit right. So that meant poetic discursions on her gleaming tresses were right out. She was not a person with tresses, nor even locks, nor shining waves—she was a person who had only *hair*.

Which! Was its own kind of fascinating, wasn't it! Corentin had never met anyone who so resisted description, and he *had* always liked a challenge.

Challenges like, "walk the lantern path if you're so keen on proving you have Talesyn's favor." Challenges like, "stand right here in the middle of the terrifying forest while I go catch something for dinner and look for water."

Challenges like, "beg the Lord of Song for a bit of awen to light this lantern."

Corentin really didn't know how Aneth managed to deal with this fear. A little gust of wind blew a leaf across the road in the corner of his eye; he yelped and then cursed a blue streak, and by the time he collected his wits, he found himself pointing one accusing finger at that leaf and enumerating all the possible scandals of its parentage and ancestry in a voice that was maybe a little louder than was advisable in the middle of a terrifying forest.

He cleared his throat, tossed his hair out of his eyes, re-settled his hat to a jaunty angle on his head, looked around to make sure nobody had seen that—good, good, not a soul in sight, that was perhaps a major perk of terrifying forests.

"This is stupid and I hate it," he told the offending leaf. "I am going to stop now." Another breeze tickled one of his hat's feathers against his nape and he had to make a very undignified noise and walk in a little circle for a minute, scrubbing his hands over the back of his neck and wriggling to get the goosebumps of adrenaline to die down so he could feel less like crawling out of his own skin.

"Aaaaaa," he said emphatically to that fucking leaf. Was he going a little mad? Perhaps he was going a little mad. Making incoherent vowel sounds at a random leaf was not the sort of madness he had envisioned for himself. He'd been hoping for something more stylish. Sexy.

Speaking of sexy, did he dare to take his boots off?

He considered this for a long moment, because the throbbing pain of his feet was the one thing keeping him from going instantly batshit with terror, but on the other hand, they really fucking hurt.

"Perhaps I shall take just one off at a time," he said to his horrible leaf friend. "Then if I keel over dead of fright, the other boot will still be on my leg, suitable for use in identifying my body."

He sat on the ground, spent several minutes attempting to wrestle the tab-and-toggle closures open with his shaking fingers, which were fear-clumsy, and weak with fright, and nearly numb with terror, and—oh, that was three identical descriptors, wasn't it? He'd have to pick just one for the poem.

The agonized relief of freeing one foot (the one *without* the fancy anklet, of course) from the boot made him groan aloud, then freeze as he looked nervously around the road and the wood again. He hummed a terrified little tune to keep his brain occupied as he rubbed his poor aching foot, and then he bounced back up. *Fuck,* it felt good to be flat-footed. The cobblestones under his feet—well, foot and boot—were warm, but he eyed the grass just by the side of the road and thought of how lovely a nice cool brook would be... He edged to the side of the road and carefully extended his bare foot to rub it blissfully on the verdant grass with a sigh. Oh, that did feel better, yes. That invigorated him greatly—which on one hand also invigorated his fear, but he was a man with one shoe and a leaf for a best friend, so really what could defeat him? Other than the hordes of ravenous monsters that were probably creeping up behind him at this very moment, their jaws slavering and dripping with hunger...

He whirled around, in a very casual and collected sort of way, just to check.

He hummed his terrified little tune again and picked up his lute, clutching it against his chest. The strings sounded a little as the belly of the lute bumped against his ribs. He scrambled the strap over his shoulders, fretted an E minor chord, and plucked a few strings.

It was not exactly *soothing*—it did not send the fear fading away as the lanterns had—but it did give him enough presence of mind that it occurred to him that being best friends with a terrifying leaf after three minutes was probably not the decision of a man who was currently in possession of all his marbles.

Don't want to come on too strong, after all, he thought hysterically, and then played another E minor chord, over and over and over, a constant up-and-down strum pattern until his brain was able to seize on the music and remember A minor, and then G, and then C and D—

"Hey, that's halfway to a song," he said to the leaf—why was he talking to a leaf? Oh, fuck it, never mind that.

The ebbing of the fear was so gradual that he didn't at first notice it—his fingers got defter, his timing and melodic instincts sharpened, he got his *mind* back. He was toying around with chord progressions and strum patterns when he noticed it and, his heart catching in his chest and skipping four or five beats in a row, he looked at the lantern in hope...

Nothing.

Fuck.

He closed his eyes in frustration, disappointment, a mere flash of despair before it was swiftly quashed by the determination to *get it,* to find the notes or the words or the melody that would unlock it and light the awen—

But that wasn't how it worked. That was how stories said it worked—and, granted, that was how he would tell the story of this one working, if he could manage it.

He had doubted, in the back of his mind, whether inspiration really did come from Talesyn or not. He had no answer either way, but the logic was undeniable—new lanterns were lit by those who the Lord of Poets had marked with his favor, and they were fueled by the inspiration of others who came after. Their dreams, their stories, their *ideas.* But the lanterns all, eventually, went dark. A hundred years after the death of someone who had lit a lantern on the path, or two hundred years, or five hundred years, the flame would begin to gutter like a candle about to drown itself in its own melted wax, and the inspiration of that person would at last exhaust itself.

No one's well of invention was limitless. It always, eventually, ran dry. Therefore, it must be something that came from within the human spirit, rather than a gift from the gods—if Talesyn had been the true source of that inspiration, then the lanterns once lit would never go out.

But it was nevertheless heartening to know that the limit of one person's invention might last longer than their lifespan did. That those favored by the Lord of Song might, when their lives ended, pass into his meadhall and sing for generations more amongst their fellows, that they might have a chance to write the songs that had gone unwritten and tell the stories that had gone untold—that although the fire wouldn't burn forever, it *would* burn as long as it needed to. Corentin's heart always ached at that thought, and it ached now, imagining Elouan singing his last song in Talesyn's hall and feeling not despair or dismay, but contentment and completion.

He found his fingers shifting to other chords, better ones, bittersweet and beautiful ones—he didn't have the words for this song yet, if words there were, but he *felt* it with his entire heart, he leaned into the music and let the music lean back into him, and he pictured Lord Talesyn's meadhall, its tall vaulted ceilings like those of the ancient chiefs, the windows spilling golden midday light amongst the gathered throng—the poets and minstrels and players and orators, those who had sought for knowledge and for the speaking of it. He shaped the image with music, described with the ringing of his lutestrings the merriment of many voices singing together, the way awed silence would spread across a crowd when truth rang out above their voices.

He imagined Elouan, who had written so many songs that so many people still loved, playing his last one in triumph and pleasure and contentment, and finally being able to sit down and rest for a time, drinking deep from Clevertongue's cups of Clevertongue's wine which was said to burn like fire coursing down the throat and taste like light and summer and joyful, *true* words on your tongue.

Corentin played for Elouan's light which had burned for so long; he played for Elouan's well-earned rest and the drink to wet his tongue; he played for another, standing up to take his place and continue the songs and stories and the speaking of knowledge; he played for Elouan getting up from the long wooden tables, smiling and unnoticed by anyone but perhaps the Lord of Poets himself, who might lay a hand on his shoulder as they passed each other, and smile at his favored one, and draw him close to kiss his shining brow which had lit the world for so long.

He played for Elouan quietly and willingly and with *satisfaction* passing from the meadhall out into... whatever was beyond it, while the music and the laughter continued on around the great fire at the center of the hall—the fire that was Talesyn's own fire, the one of which all others were mere imitations.

"Well!" said a voice from behind him, a voice like silver and the soul of poetry, a voice like the chill that ran up your spine at the sound of one perfect sentence or one perfect line of music, a voice like midday sunshine and the height of summer, a voice like sleeping embers blown softly into dancing flame, a voice like the moment of silence at the end of a song before the beginning trickle of applause that grew to a riot. The voice said, "Such a song as that is a rare thing indeed, Corentin. Have you a name for it?"

Corentin's fingers had stilled on the strings at the first word; that chill had run up his spine. Tears had come into his eyes, and his heart had leapt into his throat... And he was suddenly and painfully aware that he had on only one shoe, that he was unwashed and grimy from a couple days' trek through the woods and from sleeping on the ground, and that he'd been mad enough a few minutes ago to make friends with a fucking leaf. Perhaps the earth would do him a favor and swallow him up.

This was not at all how he had ever anticipated meeting Talesyn Clevertongue.

He cleared his throat. "I'm still workshopping the title, lord," he said, trying to sound casual. "I thought 'Ode to the Flame of Elouan', but that might be a little pretentious. Not catchy enough. You know, that sort of problem."

"Mm," said the Lord of Song, amused. "I do."

"May I—may I look upon you, lord?" He was trembling all over, trembling as he had in the very depths of forest-terror, but now it was all just longing and relief and joy and an inchoate wish to throw himself at Talesyn's feet and hug his thighs and weep for the sheer immensity of emotion.

"Oh, I wish you would," Clevertongue said, laughing. "Am I not the god of poets and players and great orators? Am I not the god for whom the very act of looking upon another—or their performance—is an act of worship and celebration?"

Corentin shuffled around and shyly looked at his god.

All red and gold was the Lorelord at first glance, and then the eye was dazzled as the red became all the colors of fire, as the gold became all the colors of light shining through a faceted jewel and breaking into a hundred thousand splinters of rainbow.

Talesyn was tall, or he seemed so—Corentin could not tell how tall he was, nor what he looked like. He could have been a sun-toasted as Aneth or as pasty as Corentin himself, or any of the hundred shades of skin that Corentin had seen on the streets of Brassing-on-Abona. He could have had any color of hair, any length, any style. He could have had any color of eyes, and in any shape. He was impossible to look upon and yet impossible to look away from—and rather than the sight striking terror and awe into Corentin's heart, as he had instinctively expected, he found himself laughing aloud in delight, as if he had witnessed the most marvelous play or heard the most marvelous song, or been told the most marvelous joke. He laughed for joy in knowledge and creation, he laughed for the delight of witnessing another's skill with words and expression.

He put his fingertips to his lips and fell silent, abashed.

Talesyn smiled at him. "I do find it heartening when one of you laughs rather than falling to your knees."

"I laughed because I am so happy to see you, lord," Corentin said, blushing.

"Yes, I know." Talesyn glanced down and smiled at Corentin's feet. "Whatever has happened to your other boot, child?"

"It's here," Corentin said, pointing to it on the ground just behind him. "They hurt my feet," he explained, indeed feeling much like a child. "But they're too nice to take off both at once."

"I see," said Talesyn, still brimming with amusement. "They are nice indeed, aren't they. I have never seen their like before." He laughed aloud, his voice ringing off the trees, which was so beautiful Corentin felt the tears come into his eyes again and rather wanted to swoon right off his aching feet.

"Teasing aside—yes, they are excellent boots," Talesyn said more seriously. "For the laughter you have brought out in me with your marvelous boots, I shall grant you a boon; for the laughter you offered from your own heart upon meeting me, I shall grant you another. For the lovely song you played, a third. Small ones, mind you," Talesyn added with a languorously indulgent smile. "On the scale of 'Lord of Song, make my boots even nicer than they already were.'"

"Oh, yes *please*."

Talesyn laughed again, softer—almost human, almost, but still exhilarating and beautiful and true—and said, "Sit down, then, and we can talk as I work."

Corentin folded to the ground right where he was standing.

The Lord of Song knelt neatly before him. He was wearing some kind of cloak or robe or something, Corentin saw now, his eyes adjusting to the glory and splendor of knowledge and music and poetry incarnate. That was the red thing, the fire-colored thing across Talesyn's shoulders. A cloak, or perhaps a coat—rather like Corentin's own, he thought with delight. Perhaps that would be a good second boon. But he'd wait and see what Silverthroat did with the boots first.

"Should I take this one off?" he said, wiggling his other foot.

"Depends," answered Talesyn, still smiling at him. "What makes the best story, to your mind?"

"Oh, good question." He regarded the boots—the one slumped beside him on the ground, the one on his foot with the anklet glittering bright in the sunshine. "Honestly, I'd probably elide the whole mess, if it were me."

"Who else is there to tell this story but you?"

"Point. No one really cares about the putting-on and taking-off of boots... I think I'll have them on," he said decisively. "Then I can skip the bit where I took the boot off in the first place, and no one will ever have to know you caught me half-shod."

He wrestled his leg back into the other boot, a process which involved much cursing and many muttered oaths, and then hisses of pain as his poor bruised foot was bound up once more in the tight leather.

Talesyn watched him, fondly amused, and when Corentin extended his feet again, the Lord of Song rubbed his hands together. "It has been some time since I bestowed a boon like this—let alone three." He held out his hands as if warming them by a fire. "Now, what shall we speak of?"

"Will lighting the lantern be too great a boon to ask for?"

Talesyn raised his eyebrow. Corentin flushed, but held his gaze. After a moment, Talesyn said, "The lantern is not as important as you seem to think it is."

Corentin said nothing.

After another very long moment, Talesyn continued. "There was a time when this section of the road was marked by only the standing stones at either end and the lanterns with them. In those days, travelers who wished to pass through the woods had to withstand the full might of my brother's fear. But over the centuries and millennia, my favored ones asked for light to guide the way and to provide respite, and I have answered their petitions. And so the godwood—or at least the road *through* the godwood—grows endurable, if not civilized." Talesyn cast his eyes to the old, darkened lantern. "The light I granted Elouan has gone out. He has passed out of my hall, as all those who enter it eventually must." In a voice that was almost gentle, he added, "Without his light, this road will not become impassable. Nor will the woods be any safer with a new one."

Corentin's cheeks stung with a blush. "Yes, my Lord. But I do have a personal interest..."

"Ah, yes, your wager."

"Clevertongue, I have dedicated myself to your path since I was old enough to sing. I cannot believe that I am utterly unfavored in your eyes."

Talesyn smiled, his eyes dancing. "There are many kinds of favor, are there not? I favor every poet, every bard, every player, all those who seek knowledge, all those who shout truth even when many are unwilling to hear it, and all those who warm their hands by my fire. I favor every person who sits in an audience and grants the blessing of their attention. But there is favor, and then there is *favor*. There *are* those, once in a generation, who are fated for me in some way. But you, alas, were not, despite your excellent boots and very, very lovely song." His voice was not unkind, his eyes still dancing with warmth, but Corentin still felt the sting of disappointment lance through him. He opened his mouth to protest, but Talesyn raised one hand in a calm, quelling gesture. "That said, your service to me has been unwavering, and I do not wish for you to think that this is a judgment on that, nor on the quality of your talents. It's merely something that *is*, in the way that fire simply *is*."

Corentin tried to speak around his plummeting heart. Tears had sprung to his eyes somewhere in there. "So I am unfit?"

"*Unfit* is a strong word. You are not unfit at all. Let us say... you have not yet been ready."

"Is it a fixed thing? Is there no recourse or appeal? Can I not earn your favor through actions, or song, or true speech, or the search for knowledge?"

Talesyn tilted his head back and forth, considering. "Perhaps. There is no one way into my favor. There are some who were born to it, fated to it—and there are some who did not come to my sight then, and it was only later, when their light revealed itself to the world, that my eye was caught. You were not born to it nor fated to it." The Lorelord shrugged. "But you chose it, so we shall have to wait and find out what you do with it and whether you might earn it. Even the gods cannot see the future."

"Shouldn't you be able to? You're said to be the god of soothsayers."

"And I am that!" Talesyn laughed. "But soothsayers are performers like any other. They do not know any more than you or I what the choices someone will make—and it is the choices of each person that affect the shape of the future. But take heart—as I said, there is the possibility that you may gain my favor in the future. Then again, there is the possibility that you may decide that you do not need it."

"I need it now," said Corentin—pleaded, really. "I need it to light the lantern. Wagers or no, this was what I promised to do. This is part of the service your priests require of each other. If I did not take on this task, then someone else would have had to. Someone else would have had to walk the lantern path and sacrifice pieces of their own inspiration to keep the fires lit."

Silence fell between them. He watched Talesyn, watched his hands. They were extraordinarily steady. The whole of him was extraordinarily steady, a fixed point in the midst of this unfixed place.

The wind rustled through the trees, the westering sun beating down upon their heads. Corentin wondered how far Aneth had gone, whether she had found water and food or been taken by the madness of the forest. Surely she of all people would be granted the mercy of the Hunter.

Talesyn smiled down at Corentin's boots. He once more rubbed his palms together—*poems, his hands are poems-*, Corentin's eyes told him before he blinked away the strange refraction of the light—and held them out again, tilting his head from side to side as if looking at the boots from several different angles. "You want to light the lantern for the sake of other travelers. You want to light the lantern for the sake of other priests. You know that this is an unpleasant task for a number of reasons, and you took it upon yourself. You were willing to make the sacrifice of your poems—your ideas, your inspiration—to keep the lanterns lit. Despite the fact that it is not a strictly necessary task, or one that I think as important as you do... I still do not wish you to think that this is an act that I am unimpressed by, nor one that I find valueless."

"I should hope not!" said Corentin. "You are the god of fire, so therefore you are the god of hospitality. As the god of hospitality—not to mention as the god of poets and players—then you should understand the value of caring for one's audience. "

Talesyn chuckled. "That is the first misunderstanding that you people seem to make. I, beloved, am not human. I have never been human. I was born of the magic of the world, the light of the sun, the heat of fire, the first line of song sung on these shores. You always seem to think that because I *seem* human in appearance to your eye that I must *be* human—that I share your priorities. The conclusions that you draw are human conclusions. Are a god's concerns necessarily identical to mortal ones?"

"But they are," Corentin insisted. "At least some of the time, they are! Is it not true that you were there to rebuff the invaders at the Battle of the Bridge, Silverthroat?" He gestured sharply down the road in the direction that he and Aneth had come from. "The fires that are lit in these lanterns are the *epitome* of human concerns. The light of inspiration is the light of civilization—is that not the most human thing possible? *The* most human of concerns? What other creature on this earth writes poetry? Or sings songs?"

"Birds," Talesyn said straight-faced, though mirth glittered in his eyes.

That same mirth-fire leapt up in Corentin's chest, and he surrendered to laughter. "Point well-taken, my lord! Nevertheless, why light these fires at all? Why light all those lanterns if, as you claim, you are free of human concerns? You must have seen *some* purpose in it—you are not the Lord of Temptations, to require no other reason than providing pleasure and indulgence to those you favor."

"Indeed I am not," Talesyn said, a wry smile curling at the corner of his mouth. "But indulgence does not belong *only* to my brother Idunet, and I do find myself easily persuaded by the requests of my favored ones. You are not wrong, however—I do have my own concerns."

Corentin thought deeply, thought what a god's concerns might be—thought specifically about what *Talesyn's* concerns might be as the god of fire, as the god of poets and the light of bardic inspiration, as the god of all those who shout the truth, as the god of the noonday sun.

At last, not entirely sure that he was guessing in the correct direction but knowing in his bones that Talesyn would not punish him for too much presumption, he asked slowly: "Is it not a good thing to have more of that light—-*your* light—in the world? Would that not be one of your concerns?"

Talesyn watched him, his eyes still smiling, and said nothing.

Corentin had been afraid for all of that day and all of the previous one, afraid of the woods, afraid of what might be lurking behind every tree... But he could not find it within himself to be afraid of his lord, even when his lord had appeared before him, even when his lord claimed that he was not human, that he did not have human concerns. Now more than ever before, he was as familiar to Corentin as the beat of his own heart or the sound of his own voice. "Is it not a good thing to have more of that light? Is that not one of your concerns, Lord Clevertongue?"

"Ah," Talesyn said, sitting back on his heels. "Now you begin to think like a god."

"I have already sacrificed much for the sake of keeping these fires lit. I am no stranger to it." Corentin met Talesyn's eyes boldly, because Aneth had been right—both her god and his appreciated boldness. "If I do not yet have your favor, Silverthroat, I accept that. I will continue to aspire towards such honor for the rest of my life, and I will hold onto the hope of one day earning it.

"But the problem before me now is this lantern. It *does* need to be lit—you say that the road won't become impassable, but... My lord, before you came, I was maddened by the fear. Just because it is *possible* to walk the road in that state doesn't mean that people can—nor that they will dare to try if they know there is such a long stretch unlit! I know it is a human concern rather than one of your own, but... I hope you will consider it, for their sake. It makes a *difference,* lord. It does." Talesyn was watching him, his eyes warm and sparkling and full of the secret knowledge of the world. Corentin went on, trying to match that pleasure and enjoyment, cajoling and coaxing because that too was one of Talesyn's areas—persuasion was an aspect of rhetoric and performance, after all. "Is there any bargain we could strike for it? The lantern lit for the price of something I could provide, or some service I could offer? Some other sacrifice you would ask of me?"

Talesyn studied Corentin for several long moments. His smile was wry and his voice laced with merriment as he murmured, "How presumptuous of you to demand to negotiate with a god! I have given you three boons already, yet you ask for another, an even greater one! One far outside the bounds of what I've offered."

"Yes," said Corentin, rueful but almost laughing—the effects of the Talesyn's sparkling humor were as potent as Ystrac's wilderness-fear. "Yes, well, my lord... My impression of you was that presumption might amuse you rather than offend."

"I am not a god of sacrifices," said Talesyn, still smiling. "It is the nature of the awen that it requires fuel in the form of your poems. As any poet knows, inspiration burns out eventually if it is not fed—but the light of inspiration could just as easily have been spread through those poems that you gave up. I have never asked you to withhold your works, nor to dispose of them—in fact, I asked for the latter. I asked for them to be shared with others, for the truth to be spoken aloud and songs sung to fill the silence. To give them up has been your choice. Your sacrifice, for the sake of a good *you* desire." Talesyn put his head a little on one side. "But I will admit... more of that light in the world is something that I do indeed value." After a moment of pensive consideration, he continued: "So—you speak of bargains." Corentin's heart skipped a beat—he hardly dared to breathe. "*If* I do this momentous thing for you, I will indeed demand some service in return. I will also impose restrictions upon you: If anyone asks what transpired between us, you must tell them the truth—in fact, you must tell them the truth even if they *don't* ask."

"What shall I say?"

"You may tell them about the boons that I have granted you, and you may tell them about the bargain that we make—if indeed we do make it. You may say that you owe me a great service, and that I did this thing as a favor to you—but *not* that I did it because of the favor I *hold* for you." Talesyn's smile broadened and he laughed softly. "In any case, I imagine that they'll be more interested in your wonderful boots then they will be in the lantern itself."

Corentin had to admit that this was probably true. Most people were not interested in thinking about the godwood if they had no need of going there. He didn't blame them. It was an uncomfortable thing to be confronted with—even the thought of it had troubled him on the long journey to the marker stone where the fear had set upon him.

But the thing that made his heart stutter in his cheest was the suggestion—conditional though it was—that Talesyn already considered the deal made. He was cooperative enough to speak of what Corentin *could* say, that his audience *would* be more interested in the boots. He spoke as if it was almost, *almost* done deal—done except for Corentin himself accepting the terms.

Corentin tried not to squirm with glee, and decided not to call attention to Talesyn's wording. "May I ask what kind of service you might require of me?"

"Now where would be the fun in that?" Talesyn's hands were still outstretched as though he were warming them at a fire. Corentin studied his boots—they didn't look any different yet, though his feet were hurting less. That alone was a very exciting prospect, if that was the magic that Silverthroat was laying on them.

"Not even a hint or an example?" Corentin leaned back on his hands, grinning. "Or perhaps a story about someone else's bargain and what they exchanged for you to do them such a favor? At least give me an idea of the scale that I'll be working with."

"I'm afraid not. There are several things still in motion, and I do not yet know how the dice will fall. As I said before: Much depends on the actions and choices of others." He looked thoughtful again for a moment. "What I can tell you is this," he said slowly. "It won't take you out of Brassing-on-Abona. Any favor-debt that I will require of you in the near future will take place there."

"The capital?" Corentin said, intrigued.

Talesyn nodded, lowering his eyes to the boots, an intent expression coming across his face momentarily.

Corentin laughed a little, relieved. "Well! I can't say I mind that hint." He considered for a moment. "Say, does it have anything to do with the theaters? You know, all of the nonsense that's been going on with those, the Edict and suchlike."

Talesyn's eyes rose to meet his again. A sly smile twinkle in his eyes. "Perhaps," he said. "Do we have a deal? A favor for you now—or rather a service, let's not get our terminology confused—and for me, a service later. And the binding promise that you will not claim to have my favor, nor obfusticate by omission the fact that you do not have it. You will tell the truth of what we have spoken here, and you will not be permitted to use it for your own gain or glory." He tilted his head a little in an allowing gesture. "Unless, of course, the song you sing of this is really spectacularly good. We shall consider any gains or glories as a result of *that* to be rightful reward for your own work and talent—fame, the acclaim of the audience, and so on."

Well, Corentin certainly couldn't ask for anything more fair than that—and it was supremely fair in his eyes. He nodded so enthusiastically that his earrings danced against his cheeks. "Agreed, lord, of course! I don't seek to trick you or mislead you. I assure you that there's no need to bind me with careful wording." He gestured to his boots. "You're giving me three boons, after all! Even without the lantern, it would be unbearably callous to cross you after such a generous gift. Hell, set aside that too—Clevertongue, I do love you. I have for many years." Corentin smiled helplessly at him. "That would be enough of a reason not to cross you: I don't *want* to."

Talesyn sat back on his heels and lowered his hands. His eyes were bright and warm. "Shall I tell you, then, what gifts I have given your already very nice boots?" Corentin nodded eagerly again, and Talesyn folded his hands neatly in his lap, his posture very straight. "Your boots are indeed terribly fine. Even I admire them. I have given them the gift of material strength, such that they will not wear out for a very long time, and I have undone the scuffs and wear that they have taken already. Henceforth the sun will not fade their color, and no stone nor road will dare to leave a mark upon them. Neither rain nor standing water will penetrate them, nor snow, nor even the cold of winter. Your feet will be as warm as though you sat by my own fire, in my own mead hall.

"No matter how many miles you walk, these boots will not hurt you. Your feet may grow sore, but that will have nothing to do with the boots themselves—that will simply be the price of miles walked. The boon is only for the boots themselves, you understand, not for the limitations of your own physiology."

"Yes, my lord," Corentin said. "Thank you very much!"

"I'm not finished," Talesyn said, his amused smile widening to a grin. He fairly well shone with pride and smugness, tipping up his chin like he was pleased to show off—and he probably was, being the god of show-offs like Corentin. "The gilt on the heels will never flake off, the laces will never break, and the stitching will never fray. Besides all that, when you wear the boots, as long as you are speaking the truth, people will be more likely to listen to you. They will *hear you*—in the sense that any song you sing will cut through the noise of even the most crowded room. It will not silence the crowd, nor will it force their attention to turn to you if they do not will it, nor magically influence them to be convinced or persuaded by what you say. But they will hear you."

Corentin noticed, distantly, numbly, that he had tears in his eyes. Had he been struck by lightning? He might as well have. "My lord..." he said weakly, and that was about all he could say.

Talesyn nodded and seemed satisfied. "Now, what will you ask for your other boons?"

Corentin didn't even have to think about it. "My coat," he blurted, blinking away his tears. He felt flattened, as though he should lay facedown on the road and grovel in thanks—yet he also wanted to leap up and dance for the joy and exhilaration of these splendid adventure. Or curl into a ball and weep from the sheer exhausting *muchness* of it all, now capped with this great gift. Plural—*these* great gifts, because he got to ask for a third. "And—"

He hardly dared say it, yet he *did* dare, because his lord rewarded daring: "And my lute."

"Ah," said Talesyn, his expression warming until it seemed as though he were blazing with pleasure-. Corentin's heart thundered in his chest. "It has been a great many years since I laid a boon on an instrument."

For this, he held out his hands, and Corentin scrambled to pull the strap of the lute over his head. As he placed the instrument in the Lord of Song's hands, the strings sounded with a single beautiful note. Corentin's hands shook as he lowered them back into his lap, watching with emotions too great for anyone to have ever invented a word for them.

Talesyn laid the lute across his lap, stroking his long fingers across the honey-colored soundboard, the simple catgut strings, the long slender neck, the tuning pegs. "A fine instrument," he said quietly, looking down at it. "It sings of the hours you have spent on it, the care with which you have handled it—and the care with which you *haven't* handled it," he added with a scolding glance at Corentin from under his eyelashes. He stroked his hands across the lute again, almost soothing, as though he was stroking a cat.

Talesyn had easily carried on a conversation with Corentin before, but now his attention was entirely fixed on the lute. The air seemed to *thrum* around them, the long grass beside the road stirring in a breeze Corentin could not feel with any of his body's senses, the dust of the road rising in thin wisps around them. "No harm shalt thou take," the Lord of Song intoned, his voice strangely resonant. It was undefinably different from before: More staggering, more beautiful, more unearthly, more true. "Thy strings shall not break, nor thy neck, nor thy body. Thy varnish shall not grow dull—thou shalt not bear even a mote of dust nor a smudge of a fingerprint, but ever shine as bright as if new-made. The notes thou playst will be true and clear, and thy strings will be gold—except in firelight when thy master is singing, and then they shall appear as wires of flame. Thou shalt never be stolen or lost or otherwise taken from him; thou shalt be beautiful in both sound and sight. Above all, of course, *thou shalt stay in tune.*"

The thrumming increased, and suddenly Corentin could feel something radiating off of the Lord of Poets, stinging like the blazing heat of a fire on wind-chilled cheeks. Talesyn seemed *made* of fire, then, or something like fire—something primal and ineffable and elemental, and yet somehow familiar and *human.*

"Thy name," said Clevertongue, the Lorelord, Songspinner, "is Avigual, Desire-for-Glory."

A chill ran down Corentin's spine and every hair on his body stood on end.

After a breathless moment, the tension eased. The thrumming died out; the breeze calmed; the dust of the road drifted back down to the cobbles.

Corentin scrambled to take off his coat.

Talesyn took it with a laugh, and handed him back the lute—Avigual.

Avigual! Not only an instrument enchanted by the Lord of Song, but *named* by him too! Corentin cradled it reverently, running his hands over it the same way that Talesyn had. The strings did indeed appear golden in the light, as if they were made of threads of sunshine, and Corentin's heart caught to see the gloss of the varnish on the lute's body and the softer luster of the tuning pegs and sound-board. And just there, on the narrow edge of one of the tuning pegs, burned into the wood in calligraphic letters and seeming to still bear a shimmer of glowing embers in their depths was written the lute's name.

Avigual, Desire-for-Glory—oh, *such* a name!

He inspected the lute closely from end to end, hardly daring to touch the strings for fear of sounding them. As long as he did not play a note, he could keep imagining what the effects of Clevertongue's gifts might be, whether it would sing as beautifully in reality as it did in his imag-ination...

But part of him—a great part of him—hesitated. Could it possibly live up to what he had imagined? Could any-thing?

He had tears in his eyes, he noticed. Several of them had fallen onto the lute, where they glittered like jewels.

Talesyn hummed to himself, not quite musical, but still beautiful enough to make Corentin's heart skip a beat and draw his eyes up from the instrument across his lap as if it had always been a thing of legend. Lord Songspinner was running his fingers across the coat and nodding to himself with, Corentin thought, an approving kind of expression.

"Coats are much the same as boots," the Lord of Song murmured. "I can lay enchantments upon it that will protect you from the weather—much as your boots will—and I can lay charms of safety upon it, so that your pockets will never be picked and so that any physical harm done to you will be turned aside, whether it is a knife in an alley or a fist in a bar fight." He looked up at Corentin from under his eyelashes and smiled. "But somehow those don't seem quite your style, do they, Corentin?"

"Not... not as such, my lord."

"What would your choice be, then, if I were to offer you one? What seems a good boon for this coat of yours?"

Corentin could not find a single thing to say for several moments. He wiped the tears from his face and collected himself. "My hands overflow with gifts already, Lorelord," he said, quiet and humble. But humility was not what Clevertongue required in his priests. He sniffed back his tears, jerked up his chin, and said, "Frankly, the coat already does a great deal to protect me from the weather—it's rather good at shedding the rain, I've found. And besides that, you've already given me boots to keep my feet warm and dry and free of blisters, and you've given me a lute like the ones carried by the bards of old."

"Technically, no, I didn't," Talesyn said, laughing. "You people only got the lute two or three hundred years ago, inherited from the peoples of the mainland, and they had it from … oh, far and far away. In any case, hardly ancient! The bards of old played lyres or drums or pipes. But I take your point."

"The boots and the loot are legendary gifts by themselves," Corentin said. Oh, he could not entirely set aside his modesty. Not in the face of something so great as all this. "To have a third would be more than I think that I've earned at this point."

Talesyn gazed at him with frank curiosity. "More than you *think you've earned?* You boast that you have my favor, enough to light the lanterns in my brother's godwood with the awen, and yet you do not feel that you are worthy of such paltry gifts as these?"

"At *this* point, yes." Corentin mustered up his sweetest smile. "I do enjoy having things to aspire towards, and from all you've said, it sounds like the coat is more achievable as a reward than your favor is—surely you, of all the gods, can understand the simple pleasures of a small reward for a day's good work? The joys of sitting beside the hearth and resting?"

"In some small part, though that's more my sister Angarat's area of expertise." His smile was a song, his eyes a pair of flames.

"Of course." Corentin shook his head. "It *is* a good coat, and… and having a third gift does make it a tricolon—which is the right shape for this sort of thing in a song or story..."

"Certainly, certainly," said Talesyn, amused. "So you don't want a gift, but you do want a gift."

"It's not so much that I *want a gift*," Corentin protested weakly. "It's really just for the sake of the song. On another day, sometime in the future, if you feel like I've done well enough and that you'd like to insist on pressing a gift upon me, then you can come back and make the coat as fine as it should be."

"But of course," said the Lord of Song dryly. "Well then, what should we give you that is a gift but not a gift? For the sake of the song, of course," he added with a perfectly straight face.

Corentin was so muddled up and addled by honors and gratitude and overcoming emotion that he could barely think. "It—it should be something small, appropriate for a first gift, so that in the song, I can build up to the lute and say it was the third gift, as the boots are clearly the second."

"If I might make a suggestion?"

"Yes?" Corentin realized, with a sudden flash of mortification that cut through the haze of astonishment, that he had practically been telling Lord Clevertongue *what he ought to do*. Perhaps the ground would do him the courtesy of swallowing him up. Perhaps Ystrac's hunt might honor him by stampeding over him until he was jelly.

But Talesyn was still smiling. "If you think it would be *dramatically appropriate,* dearest Corentin, how would you like your coat to have a little glamour on it? One that has no effect on you nor on the audience around you... Other than the fact that it shall appear to them to be the very finest coat that they have ever seen—only that, nothing more."

Corentin, still blushing, cleared his throat and attempted to set aside his embarrassment. Boldness, that's what Talesyn favored. "The only thing I'd be worried about is whether it would put me in danger of being pickpocketed or mugged in an alley. Regardless of what its actual value is, having the *appearance* of the finest coat in the world will make it seem... expensive. But—no, the only thing of value that I have besides the coat is the lute and the boots."

"And you don't want the boon on this to be too extravagant," said Talesyn, straight-faced. "Because of the structure of the story. Amongst other things."

"Right," said Corentin, his blush returning in full force.

Talesyn laughed at him, not unkindly. "By all means, then, let it be a pickpocketable coat. For now, at least—you'll have to be just as careful as usual. But as I do not like my gifts going astray to those who did not rightfully receive them, I will enchant the coat itself such that it too cannot be taken from you by force. Your money might be stolen, or your books, or your bag, or whatever else you carry—but the coat itself will be safe... Unless you give it to someone else, of course, or lose it in a game of cards, or forget it in a mail coach."

"Thank you, my lord," Corentin managed to squeak. The most beautiful coat in the world, entirely his own, unable to be taken from him? Oh yes, that would do wonderfully.

Less distracted now, he watched the Lorelord work, watched his hands as they stroked over the thin, use-softened leather of the coat. All the scuffs and visible marks of wear faded away, and the leather took on a subtle *something*, as though glistening with fairy magic. The color became deeper and richer, the shadows velvety and the highlights almost iridescent. The fabric lining took on a shimmering luster, as if it had been woven with threads of gold and silver.

When Talesyn was finished, he handed Corentin the coat with a ceremonial air, his eyes twinkling like embers in ash. "I believe you will find this more than satisfactory."

Corentin rested his lute across his lap and wrestled his arms into the sleeves of the coat. It fit him as well as it ever had—it didn't feel like the dimensions of it had been adjusted at all. But oh, the *color!* From up close, the color was fascinating, entrancing. Corentin found that he could not stop touching it either, running his hands over the soft leather outside and the now-silken inner lining. He couldn't decide whether it was nicer to look at or to touch—he shifted it this way and that in the sunlight so he could see how it glimmered and shone, rubbed it between his fingertips as he tried valiantly to come up with words to describe the texture of something that was nothing but pure joy to brush against.

"Stand up," said Talesyn. "There is more to beauty than color and texture."

Corentin obeyed, holding the neck of the lute as he rose. "My feet still hurt," he remarked with interest. "But they were bruised and blistered already, and—oh, I suppose you did say you were only enchanting the boots."

Talesyn inclined his head once. "Now walk."

Corentin took a few steps, testing out the boots, then whisked around in a way that had always made the skirts of his coat flare out in a dramatically pleasing fashion.

The movement still made the coat flare in a dramatically pleasing fashion—not much change there that he could notice, except for the improving effect of the color and luster. The gold spangles on the bottom hem caught the light *splendidly,* though.

"Try saying something," said Talesyn, smiling to himself. "Something momentous or profound."

Corentin didn't have to think for more than a moment.

He already was standing with excellent posture, his feet arranged neatly one before the other, his head held high. He had spent years closely watching the great performers of the city—the players, poets, bards, orators—and he had devoured every scrap of technical knowledge he could glean from his watching. He'd done this since he'd been old enough to know that what they did... and that what they had was something he wanted. He had learned how to perform, how to pose and declaim, how to project any emotion into his voice and bearing for his audience. He had *earned* and fought for all of that—and now, too, he had his wonderful coat and his even more wonderful boots, and a lute right out of legend.

He met Clevertongue's eyes boldly, took off his hat briefly so he could lift Avigual's strap over his head and settle it on his shoulders, the weight comfortable. "Lord of Poets, Lord of Flame, I have been yours all my life, and I will be yours even beyond death. But before that death comes to me, I swear on this lantern—on every lantern on this road, and by the flames that burn within them—I *will* earn your favor."

And then, as he spoke, the skirts of the coat *billowed* as if in a gust of perfectly timed wind.

Corentin looked down at them as they did, then jerked his gaze back up to Talesyn, his jaw dropping open with delight, all words stolen from his tongue.

Talesyn was still smiling to himself, as smug as a fox. "How's that?"

Corentin shook himself a little, changed his posture, and said experimentally, "Lord judge, stop this trial! I have discovered the identity... of the *murderer*."

The coach billowed magnificently again. Corentin made a strangled, embarrassing noise and nearly burst into tears again.

"Yes, I thought you'd like that," said Talesyn, clearly feigning modesty.

"Thank you, lord," Corentin said helplessly. "Thank you. Oh, Clevertongue! Oh, my lord, thank you!"

"One would almost think that you like the coat better than the lute and the boots," Talesyn said wryly. "Wear it in good health, my dear, and I shall look forward to your... shall we say, *courtship* for my favor."

Corentin made another little strangled sound and nodded energetically. He was trembling again, he noticed distantly—his earrings and bracelets and the spangles of his coat all jangling wildly again.

Talesyn's face grew serious, and he turned to the lantern hanging from the hook on the post.

In a low voice, he said, "And now for the rest of it." He raised his hands to waist height, his palms facing up in nearly the same gesture that he'd used when he had handed Corentin the lute and the coat, as if he were offering something or outstretching his hands to receive it. His eyes—what Corentin could see of his eyes, in any case—glinted and flickered with fire.

Talesyn spoke.

Corentin could not hear the words, but they rang through his bones like a rumbling of the earth, like the air itself had become an instrument from which Talesyn could pluck notes as easily as he might strum a lute or harp or dulcimer.

Corentin wanted to fall to his knees, wanted to burst into song in awe and reverence for this moment—but the right song was the one thrumming through the air and earth and his very bones, not one that could be played on any mortal instrument or sung with any mortal voice.

The wind stopped—the *world* stopped, or it felt as though it did, as if all of existence had paused to listen and witness.

Talesyn spoke again, his voice no longer terrible and fearsome, but as gentle as a lover whispering to his love. "Fire, awake."

These words, Corentin heard. They brought tears stinging to his eyes, his heart wrenching as if these were somehow the most beautiful two words that could ever be spoken.

There was no moment of delay. The fire awoke gradually but steadily to Talesyn's command, a tall narrow flame like that of a candle with a too-long wick. The flame was perhaps the length of Corentin's hand from heel to fingertip, and the light it gave was a newborn sun's pure gold—and as distant and impersonal as the sun too, inhuman and strange, though it was as warm and vibrant as all the others in the lanterns along the road.

It was only now that he was looking at this one, so obviously alien, that Corentin realized with a dawning awe that the flames in all the other lanterns had been unique as well, each distinct from the rest. They were strange and wonderful—yet he had perceived them initially as all the usual shades of red, orange, golden, white, blue.

Talesyn stood silently for a long moment, solemnly regarding the lantern and its burning flame of awen.

Corentin drifted a step closer. In a reverent whisper, as if the flame would be disturbed by a voice speaking too loud and too soon, he asked, "Is that that one yours, lord?"

"Every flame of every fire is mine."

"Yes, of course." But then, because Clevertongue liked a clever tongue (and a bold mind and the speaking of truth), he said, "But *this* one, this fire of inspiration—is this one yours?"

Slowly, Talesyn turned his gaze to study Corentin, piercing him to the soul with his eyes.

After what seemed an eternity, the serious expression cracked, and a hint of a smile returned to the corner of the god's mouth. "With insight such as that," he said, his voice warm with approval, "and with clear sight such as that, and with bold speech such as that... you may be closer to my favor than either of us thought an hour ago." He put his head a little on one side. "What fierce competition there is in this generation. I do wonder now whether my favor will fall to you or to the other."

"The other?"

"Your rival for my affections, as it were," Talesyn said, the flames in his eyes flickering with mirth.

CHAPTER THREE

H E WOULD BE FINE so long as he stayed on the road, Aneth thought decisively as she stepped beyond the treeline and into the green. The fear throbbed within her, scraped along her nerves—her hands would have shaken with it, if she hadn't been so accustomed to her lord's gifts. For fear was a gift—fear was what kept the mind sharp and the muscles strong when they otherwise would have failed, exhausted. Fear was a rampart against hubris and arrogance, a reminder that there were things in the world greater than you, that although your arrows might be sharp and your eye keen, there were yet those in the wood—in the world—who would match you, who would stand against you, who would not submit.

Without fear, there was no respect, no politeness, no reason to cleave close to friends and family against the wilderness and chaos... And wasn't that really what made civilization? Corentin would have claimed that it was his lord's gift that were the beginnings of civilization—fire and poetry and inspiration—but in truth, Ystrac and Talesyn were but two sides of one coin. The Hunter and the Poet, the forces of wild, untrammeled chaos and of beautiful, artistic, intentional order. The wilderness without, and the warm fireside within, and all that came with each.

Aneth walked, smiling, into the forest. The birds sang above her, the sunlight cast dapples of light down through the leaves. The underbrush was thick, but Aneth found paths through it, stepping carefully—her bow was in her hand, an arrow nocked, her ears pricked for any sound that was not her own breathing or the soft crunch of leaves under her feet or the singing of the birds.

She found the brook first, a trickle of water at the bottom of a steep, rocky slope—but here the thick underbrush assisted her again, for she was able to pick her way down with her hand on the trunks or stems of strong-rooted shrubs and slender trees. The brook was narrow enough to jump across and clear as anything. A taste of the water told her that it was clean—or clean enough to be tolerated, clean enough that they probably wouldn't fall ill from drinking it—and the old brown leaves lying at the bottom made the gentle rills flash brassy-gold in the sun. Aneth drank deep, then filled her waterskin, murmuring a brief thanks to the Lord of the Greenwood for any part he may have taken in leading her here. She washed her face, slipped off her shoes and stockings to dip her feet briskly in the cool water, and undid the toggle-closures at the front of her jerkin and tunic so she could untie her breast-band. After a moment's thought, she undid her trousers so she could replace her breechclout as well, splashed water perfunctorily between her legs and under her arms and breasts to get rid of most of the smell, and replaced her breastband and breechclout and stockings with the spare set from her bag. As she rinsed out the dirty ones, she kept her eyes lifted, scanning the forest around—though a brookside was as safe a place as there was ever going to be in the woods. Water was necessary for all creatures, and so if there were anything that came upon her—a wolf, an elk, a boar—it would leave her be as long as she let it be too. They would mind their own business, take the water they required, and move along in silence. Here in the godwood of Ystrac, of all places, that was a cer-tainty—though not enough of one to let her guard down. One never did, in the forest.

Laundry finished, she wrung out her clothes and stuffed them in her bag—no time to lay them out to dry here, and it'd go faster when she was back on the road anyway, where the sun beating down on the cobblestones made the air warmer and drier than it was in the damp, shady forest.

She picked up her bow and her full waterskin, took an-other draft from the running brook, and clambered back up the hill. It was always easier to go up than it was to go down, she'd found.

At the top of the hill, she heaved herself up onto her feet and regarded the terrain. There was still dinner to be found.

Perhaps an hour's patient work netted her a fine, fat pheasant. She smiled as she collected it and tied it by its feet to her belt so her hands would be free, and then she made a casual salute into the forest. "Thanks and respect to you, Hunter," she murmured, her heart thrumming with comfortable, familiar fear, and then she turned—

And her heart nearly leapt out of her throat.

Ystrac stood behind her.

He was perhaps a dozen feet away, and stood nearly a dozen feet tall—and that wasn't counting the antlers springing from his head. Or perhaps they were branches, winter-bare? His shoulders were broad, his hands massive. He carried a club on one shoulder, and his clothes seemed both ragged and splendid—in one moment, like mossy, brownish-green half-rotted fabric, and in the next like the many-colored splendor of full-flowered spring or fiery autumn.

His face was as strange—as terrifying as a slavering wolf, as beautiful as a gold-glinting brook or an unexpected sea of bluebells in the undergrowth.

Aneth had never been so frightened of anything in all her life. Her mouth went dry. Her hands, so accustomed to fear, trembled. She silently fumbled at her belt to free the pheasant and held it out.

Ystrac did not move. His face was so, so strange—if you could even call it a face. His hands were strange too, and his bare legs below the ragged hem of the fabric-or-whatever that was belted, kilt-like, around his hips. She could not tell anything about his expression; she could not even determine if he was looking at her or off into the distance.

Of course he was looking at her. He wouldn't have appeared to her if he were not looking.

When he did not take the pheasant or otherwise make any other gesture to suggest that he was concerned about it, she tied it back to her belt with shaking hands.

She offered him the waterskin, and at this too he showed no reaction.

She offered her bow, which she had made herself from a length of yew she had taken from the godwood the first time she had ventured within it, young and bold and as determined to claim what she knew was hers—to *give* herself unto what she knew was hers—as Corentin was with his own quest.

Three things she had claimed from the sacred godwood: the yew stave, the water, the pheasant.

The Lord of the Wilds made no motion to take her bow, gave no indication he had so much as noticed her, but for the fact that he stood before her.

She breathed through the terror, the pressing sense of danger, the animal-memory in the back of her mind screaming that a *predator* was standing before her.

Without a doubt, Ystrac was a predator. But then, so was she. She walked the woods in silence and killed when she needed to, either to protect herself or feed herself.

He seemed to have no wish to speak of his business with her, if he had any beyond this. Aneth had no more with him either, now that she had offered back those things she had taken. But then, she had never taken anything from the godwood without thanking Ystrac afterwards. For the yew stave in particular, she had also asked permission and listened to the quiet noises of the forest even before she'd cut it, in case he had any objection. He hadn't—she had cut it, she had walked out of the wood unscathed.

So Aneth nodded politely and stepped around him, giving him a wide berth.

The fear spiked up in her heart as she turned her back on him—one *never* turned one's back on a predator, except to run.

She did not run. With the pheasant swinging at her hip, the waterskin sloshing on its strap over her shoulder, and her yew bow in her hand, she walked at a calm pace in the direction of the road, no slower or faster than she would have walked otherwise.

Ystrac followed her.

He made no sound, of course—the leaves did not crunch under his feet as he stepped, nor did twigs snap as he passed through the underbrush, nor did the branches above rustle or catch on his antlers. But Aneth felt him behind her, watching her, following. The hair rose on the back of her neck, and a cold trickle of sweat ran down her spine.

She walked as silently as she could. She did not look back over her shoulder. She knew he was there, and he knew that she knew. Every nerve in her body sang *run, run, run*—but what need did she have to run from the Lord of the Wilds? Would it do her any good? She almost laughed at the thought—well, would it? If the Hunter chose to turn against her, here in the heart of his own godwood, what hope did she have?

But he wasn't turning on her—he was only following. He was... The remaining mirth from her previous almost-laugh alchemized into a smile, a *blush*. The Hunter was hunting *her*—following her, tracking her through the forest. And oh, he was being rather gentlemanly about it, wasn't he? Not making any sudden movements, not speaking, not calling up the kind of terrors of the wilderness that would drive even her mind, so well-practiced and comfortable with fear, to the breaking point.

He was just following, polite and stately and dignified, the ritual of a hunt enacted as gently and courteously as was possible.

Oh, she was drenched with fear-sweats, but an unself-conscious grin was spreading over her face with every step she took. Her shoulders squared, her chin lifted, pride and honor and joy clasping hands with the fear in her heart and swinging them round like a lively country-dance at one of the festivals in her brother's village.

She did not look over her shoulder. She did not break into a run. She opened her heart to the fear and let it set her hands to shaking, let it make her knees watery, let it sharpen her until she was as keen as a shard of new-shattered glass.

And she smiled, beaming out at the forest, wishing that every rabbit and fox and stag and boar might stop and see that it was she who had the honor of the Hunter's choice. Oh, she was as smug as any village maiden who'd been asked for a dance by the earl's handsome son.

As they neared the road, she could hear music faintly in the distance—the sweet notes of the lute, and the rise and fall of Corentin singing, though she was too far to distinguish any words or even the melody.

Ystrac laid his hand on her shoulder, and she nearly jumped out of her skin again, her fear catching on laughter as she turned and looked up at him, smiling warmly.

His face was as terrible as the sunrise, seen from a cliff overlooking the green expanse of forest. It was as beautiful as a single arrow shot true, striking the heart of a white stag and felling it instantly. It was as kind as a clouding breath in the cold of winter; it was as stern as a tree in springtime laden with flowers and swarming with honeybees.

He said nothing to her, but he set his club on the ground, leaning it against a tree, and from a fold of his clothing he withdrew something and held it out to her. She looked down—his hand was strange and inhuman, nearly twice the size of hers, if not bigger—but what lay in his enormous, weather-roughened palm was as human as anything she carried with her. It was a pouch, perhaps the size of her fist, soft sand-brown leather in a simple design with a flap closure, and it was fat with whatever filled it. The flap bore a markedly clumsy embroidery design, picked out in thick linen thread of white and green and black and mulberry. The stitches were all different lengths, different angles, unsteady—it really looked like nothing so much as something that her brother's littlest daughter might have produced as her first practice embroidery.

Aneth took the pouch. It was deceptively heavy in her hand.

Ystrac nodded once, turned, and vanished behind a tree.

She looked down at the pouch again, at its clumsy, messy stitches—such a small thing, from such a large hand… She wondered suddenly, her heart melting in her chest, whether it had indeed been Ystrac's own hand which had shaped those stitches.

She opened the flap of the pouch. Within, a handful of blackcurrants shone like the pretty glass beads on one of the necklaces her brother had bought for his wife. They were rich purple-black, so perfectly ripe and fat with juices that Aneth's mouth watered instantly. She brushed her fingertips over them—oh, yes, the absolute peak of ripeness, the kind of ripeness that could fade within hours, especially on a warm summery day like this one. They'd have to be eaten immediately.

She'd share them with Corentin, she decided easily.

She smiled down at them, pride and joy welling in her heart until even the fear was almost drowned out. A roast pheasant, and half a handful of blackcurrants for dessert. That was as princely a supper as Aneth could have imagined—what could be better than that? And even after the berries were gone, she would still have the pouch itself to treasure and remind her of this day.

She ought to tuck the pouch away—nestle it in the wet laundry in her bag to keep the berries cool—oh, and wrap it in broad leaves to protect the leather from the damp—but she could not bear to. Not just yet. She held the pouch in her hands as she headed towards Corentin's music, glancing down to smile at it again when she wasn't scanning the forest around for dangers or watching her step for uneven ground. She made less effort to keep her steps silent now, as the ever-louder music was covering her noise. She had already won her quarry, in any case.

Just before she stepped out of the treeline, it struck her how *beautiful* Corentin's playing was—and she found the fear melting away entirely, just as it had when they'd approached one of the lanterns. But before the affected area had been limited to a dozen feet around the lantern, and she was thirty or forty feet away from Corentin...

She brushed aside the last branch, coming into view of the road, and was struck once more by twin lightning bolts of shock and amazement. Corentin wasn't alone. He sat on the ground with his lute across his lap, plucking away at a lovely song—a *bawdy* song, she realized a moment later with a rush of mirth. A bawdy tavern song, elevated to loveliness.

The music filled the air like sunlight shimmering through the morning mist, and Aneth's feet stopped as she listened, fascinated and astonished. The world seemed to shift around her as she marveled at what a song could do when it was sung differently. Just a bawdy tavern song like a hundred other bawdy tavern songs, but the care and artistry with which Corentin played it and sang it made it sound... *special.* New! Not romantic, for it wasn't a romantic song, but beautiful, lively, full of joy and delight in the simple wonder of having a body that could feel pleasure in so many different ways, from so many different things. The framing, contrasted with the content of the song, was so unexpected that it tickled her brain like the best and most surprising joke, and she felt herself caught on the edge of delighted laughter.

But Corentin (she thought again, shaking off the web of fascination the song had momentarily caught her in) was not sitting alone.

Another sat with him, one knee drawn up, one elbow resting easily on it. His cloak was as red as flame, as red as the noon sun when the air was clouded with smoke. His face and form were as strange as Lord Ystrac's had been, but she could tell he was smiling at Corentin—and she could hear him humming along, and she could see his fingers tapping out the beat against his knee, and she could hear with something beyond her ears that there was more music in the air than just what came from Corentin's lute.

Lord Talesyn—Songspinner, Clevertongue, Corentin's lord—glanced away from him and looked at Aneth, turned his warm smile on her. Gestured her forward.

She duly went forward, her mind blank now except for a sense of incredulous wonder, and a swell of pride on Corentin's behalf.

"An audience arrives," spoke the Songspinner in a voice that did strange things to Aneth's nerves and muscles and sinews. It was as warm as a fire—but the fire in the hearth of a friend's house, familiar and welcoming but yet... *not hers*. Not the fire, not the hearth, not the house. Not him.

Corentin's song twanged to a stop as he whipped around. "Aneth! Oh, thank goodness—have you been driven mad? Oh, and you found dinner!"

She nodded politely to Lord Talesyn; he returned it with a small incline of his head, studying her. "I did find dinner, and I am not driven mad," she said, stepping through the long grass and onto the road. She looked first at the lantern and saw it blazing with a light that made her eyes cross and water—she had to blink and shake her head and look away, down at Corentin instead.

His coat *surely* hadn't been like that before, had it? It... looked somehow the same, but entirely different. As splendid as a fairy prince—and his *boots!*

"You look nice," she said, fascinated again twice over. "You're all glittery."

Corentin flung out his arms, laughing delightedly. "Aren't I just! Do you like it? What sort of nice do I look? Be detailed, please, it'll be weeks before I find a mirror good enough to see myself properly—it's for the song I'm going to write, you know."

She didn't much fancy herself good at the sort of details that might go in a song—but she felt the rough threads of the terrible embroidery on the pouch of berries in her hands (*was* it Lord Ystrac's own work?), and she thought that even an unskilled gift might be accepted and considered deeply touching, if it was given sincerely. She looked hard at Corentin and tried her very, very best to come up with words. "Once I saw the ostler at an inn currying a horse—I think it was a noble lord's horse. It was a blood-roan and he brushed it until you could almost see your face reflected on its flank. That's what you look like."

"A shiny horse?" Corentin asked dubiously.

"It was a really pretty horse," she said, a little defensive. "But I meant—your coat is all bright and glittery and splendid like that. And once the ostler got all the tack on, it had jingly bells and bright brass and gold, and an embroidered saddleblanket, and tassels on the bridle, and it kept arching its neck and prancing like it was proud of how fine it looked."

"I look like a shiny, vain horse?" Corentin asked, even more dubiously.

"A destrier, surely," Talesyn said, leaning back on one hand. "The bright-brushed blaze of the red roan, its brave rider bloodied, fleeing the fray to fight again some future day."

Corentin perked up. "Oh yes. Vocabulary and alliteration can make anything sound nice, can't it!" He grinned at her. "Thank you, Aneth, I shall use that."

"I didn't come up with the words, though," she said hesitantly.

But Lord Talesyn only laughed, and Corentin shook his head, smiling. "Arranging words is the easy part," Corentin said. "Picking the image is trickier. Words are just... puzzle pieces. Putting them together is more... scientific. Or mathematical. You know, counting the metrical feet and building a rhyme scheme and so on. Figuring out what phrase alliterates most beautifully." Aneth did not in fact know about that, but she nodded.

"My dear, we've surely talked of our own interests long enough," Lord Talesyn said, amusement dancing in his voice. "And I'm sure the lady can deduce the rest of our tale from the careful inventory she has taken of your gifts and the lantern. But to my eye, she seems to have stepped out of the woods like the hero of her own tale, and perhaps we should ask her how she came by that marvelous pouch she's clutching so ardently."

"Oh!" Corentin said, looking her over. "Did you have an adventure?" He glanced over at the woods and shuddered. "Actually, I'll be more surprised if you tell me that you managed to avoid adventure entirely, walking off into the godwood like that."

"I... didn't avoid adventure, no." She looked down at the pouch in her hands. "I encountered my lord."

"Chatty bunch today, aren't they," Corentin said immediately and ruthlessly; Lord Talesyn laughed again. "How was it? Don't tell me anything you don't want put into a song, otherwise I'll get so excited when I'm writing it down that I'll forget what was supposed to go in and what wasn't."

"I don't think there's really enough for a whole song," Aneth said softly, suddenly feeling very shy—not as much of Corentin, but of his lord and the strange, unfamiliar energy emanating from him. The sense of *attention,* of being *watched...* Oh, that sparked a kind of fear she had never encountered before, one that made her tongue clumsy and brought the blood rushing to her cheeks and forced her eyes down, unable to look at either of them.

"May I see?" Corentin asked gently, holding out his hand a little. Not enough to be reaching for the pouch as if he expected her to hand it over, but a gesture of offering—that his palm would be there if she wished, and easily denied if she didn't.

She hesitated, brushing her thumbs over the embroidery again, and handed it to him.

He took it carefully—as carefully as she would have handled his lute if he'd asked her to hold it—and studied it closely. Lord Talesyn leaned over to look as well, that singeing fire-flicker of amusement softening to interest and the strange, unfamiliar fear ebbing from of Aneth's mind like the falling tide.

"The Lord of the Wilds gifted you this?" Corentin asked, his voice low, almost reverent.

"Yes," Aneth said.

Lord Talesyn's smile broadened suddenly. "It has been many years since my brother granted his favor. Hail and honor to you, my lady." He inclined his head to her again, a little deeper and more formal and solemn than the one which he had greeted her with.

"What's in it?" Corentin said, weighing it. "May I open it?"

"Berries. And yes," said Aneth.

Corentin flipped open the pouch and made a quiet sound of admiration at the shining mound of blackcurrants inside. "Well! That seems a gift perfectly suited to you, somehow."

He closed it again, smiling, but before he could hand it back to Aneth, Talesyn reached out and touched the embroidery, then laughed under his breath—not cruelly, but in that way that siblings had for one another. "Oh, you must be special indeed," Talesyn said, turning his terrible, terrifying attention back to Aneth with a flick of his fire-eyes. His voice was suddenly richer, more musical, more wrenching—so complex and multilayered that Aneth wanted to shut her eyes tight and turn away and gaze at... at something *simple,* like the veins on the underside of a leaf that began stem-strong and branched out and branched out until they were as thin and fine as spider-silk. Or—her mind landed on the brassy-gold flash of the brook rippling in the dappled sunlight through the branches. She clung to that image, to the feeling of the cool green-scented air in her mouth, to the sound of the forest floor crunching under her shoes, to the throb of *proper* fear in her chest and racing along her veins. No, she didn't like Lord Talesyn's fear at all—it dulled her, slowed her, tied her up in knots. It frightened her, and the feeling of being frightened of fear only made it worse and worse.

She swallowed hard. "Why do you say that, my lord?" she asked, her voice rasping and quavering, but she forced herself to meet Lord Talesyn's eyes boldly, for both her god and Corentin's appreciated boldness.

Lord Talesyn's fingers brushed again over the embroidery. "You already guessed, I suspect, that this is made by his own hand."

She had, but to hear it spoken aloud, to hear it *con-firmed*... that was something else. She blushed and dropped her eyes.

"It is not often," the Lord of Song continued, "that I or my siblings deign to stray so far beyond our purview, even for a simple gesture such as this. Of all my siblings, Ystrac is the last whom I would expect to turn a hand to needle-work."

"I am honored twice over," Aneth mumbled, clenching her fists into hands in her lap to stop them from shaking.

"*I* didn't get anything half so cute," Corentin said, pouting at Lord Talesyn.

"*You*, my dear, have not yet earned my favor," said the Lorelord with a wry quirk of what would have been an eyebrow on anyone actually human—Aneth's eyes watered a little and her vision blurred as her eyes tried to parse what seemed like both a string of notes sung aloud or a flourish of ink on a page. "And, need I remind you, I have been indulgent enough to *light the awen for you*."

Corentin glanced up at the lantern, blinking. "Oh yes." He blinked then at Talesyn, wide-eyed and guileless, his pout returning and redoubling. "Will you give me cute things when I earn your favor?"

Lord Songspinner laughed so loud it rang off the trees and reverberated through the ground—Aneth clapped her hands over her ears and shut her eyes tight, feeling rather nauseated. *Deeply* nauseated, actually, her stomach did not feel at all well...

Corentin didn't seem to be affected in the slightest—in fact, cracking one eye open, Aneth saw he had straightened his back and shoulders and half-closed his eyes in pleasure, as if he were a cat arching its back into a stroke and leaning hard into a scritch behind its ears.

Aneth shut her eyes again and tried to breathe past her roiling stomach.

Once blocked off, she could not bear to open her eyes or ears again. She found herself scrunching smaller and smaller under the weight of that horrible *attention*—thousands of eyes looking at her, thousands—burning into her, branding her skin with fire and *eyes*—

It lasted for... who knew how long. It felt like an eternity. It must have been only another minute or two in reality. And then, abruptly, that horrible, horrible attention eased and ebbed and vanished like mist.

She still felt sick and shaky, weak enough to want to cry and hug her knees to her chest and bury her face away from the world.

A weight was laid in her lap, and then she felt a warm, human touch on her wrist. "Aneth," she heard Corentin say, muffled by her palms pressed over her ears. "Aneth, he's gone now, it's all right."

She swallowed hard several times and, with a massive effort of will, cracked open an eye again. They were alone. The sun was westering out of Brassu's hours, easing fully into the golden hours of Ystrac, who ruled the late afternoon and very early evening before the sky purpled and bruised and passed along into the hands of Idunet, lord of temptation and the twilight.

She lowered her hands slowly. Corentin laid his hand on her shoulder, stroked firmly and companionably, which went a long way to settling her nerves, though it didn't do much for her stomach. A little campfire burned nearby—a regular fire, a *mortal* fire, one that didn't strike dread into her heart like the thought of looking at the Lord of Flame.

"My lord offers his most gallant apologies," Corentin said. "He said to tell you that it has been many years since Lord Ystrac found one worthy of his favor, and many, many more years on top of that since my lord himself had any call to speak with one of you. He said that he'd forgotten how strikingly unpleasant and discordant Ystrac's kin often find him. He advises that eating a few of your berries might help."

"There's not that many," Aneth said, closing her eyes and breathing slow and steady against her nausea. She wanted nothing so much as to curl up in the grass and shut her eyes tight again and stay very, very still until the quivery, shaky feeling passed. She fumbled for the waterskin, uncapped it with hands that felt too weak to grip anything, and lifted it unsteadily to take a few sips. The cold water bloomed down her throat and hit her stomach with a sensation that was both good and very bad. She took a few more deep breaths and hung her head.

Corentin gently took the waterskin from her, sipped himself, capped it again, and set it aside.

"I was going to—" She swallowed hard. Oh, she did feel sick. "I was going to save them for us to have after dinner."

"What? Me? Share *your* berries that you got as a gift from *your* lord? I think not, my lady! You should eat every one of them yourself and enjoy them. They were for *you.*"

She tried to argue with him, but he kept on cajoling her, kicking his feet up and demanding that she look at his most wonderful boots, jumping up and swishing his coat at her while saying, "No, look here, look at this, look what it does!" (It swished, it was swishy; Aneth was perhaps a little too woozy to properly appreciate whatever nuance of it Corentin was trying to express to her), pointing emphatically at his lute and spluttering wordlessly in between telling her, incomprehensibly, "Avigual, it's Avigual; look, it's written right here—*Avigual!*"

"What's Avigual?"

"Its *name!* Eat your little berries, woman, I have gifts enough myself!" He sat back down on the cobbles and glared at her until she opened the pouch and, slowly, put one of the blackcurrants between her lips.

It burst on her tongue like... well, like the best fucking blackcurrant she'd ever tasted, tart and delicious, and sweeter than currants would normally be. Corentin would probably have poetic metaphors for it.

He made a satisfied noise and strummed his lute, picking out a cheery little tune with deft fingers that seemed to dance like butterflies across the strings and from one chord-shape to another. It was a very fine lute, Aneth reflected, eating another currant or two and listening with the same relief as sinking into a piping hot bath—or, no, better yet, the pleasure of getting *out* of the piping-hot bath after sitting in it too long, the pleasure of feeling cool air washing over tender, heat-plumped skin.

"Well?" Corentin said a few minutes later, raising an eyebrow at her. His hands continued to play, as if his attention was irrelevant to their work. "Was my lord right? Did they help?"

She nodded—she did feel much better. "I didn't know your lord could... do that."

"Do what? Tell you about berries?"

"Make me afraid like that."

Corentin cocked his head, inquisitive. "How so?" His hands played on—so funny and strange how they seemed entirely disconnected from him. The conversational tone of his voice and the expression on his face was so different than that which the music suggested.

"I don't know. I've never felt... that kind of fear."

"You're pretty used to fear."

"Yeah, but not like—not like *that*."

"What was it like, then?" His hands, unbidden, without even a glance, switched to a different tune. Aneth marveled a little to herself.

"It was like..." she said, watching almost hypnotized or entranced as his hands danced and flitted across the shimmering strings. "A bad kind of fear. Not like I was being hunted, like I was being watched. I felt like I was going to be sick in the grass. Might have, if he'd laughed again. I'd never heard of... that. Not from the Lord of Song, you know?" She shifted uncomfortably, scratched at the back of her neck. "Didn't know any of the other gods had anything to do with fear, other than mine."

"Oh!" Corentin said, his hands stilling briefly. He grinned at her. "Well, of course mine would! Stage fright! He was giving you *stage fright!*" His grin melted suddenly into sympathy. "Oh, goodness, Aneth, you poor dear! You've never even had it before, have you? No wonder you looked so green around the gills!"

She blinked at him.

"It's normal," he assured her, his hands resuming their music—now a soothing, mellow kind of song. "Everyone gets it, but it becomes easier with practice. You were probably terrified the first time you came into the godwood, right? And now you're still afraid, but it's not driving you batty." He nodded solemnly. "Whereas you leave me alone here for three minutes without the lantern lit, and I start making friends with a leaf, and then my lord catches me with one boot off, yelling at my leaf friend. Very undignified. Stage fright is just the same—*dreadful* when you're new to it, feels like you're fucking *dying*, but after a while it's just sort of... invigorating. Keeps you on your toes."

Huh. Strange. "I couldn't bear that again," she said, shaking her head. "That was the worst thing I've ever felt."

He nodded sagely, a smile twinkling in his eyes. "Well, that's why you're one of Ystrac's, I suppose. And I couldn't bear to be left alone on an unlit road in the godwood again. I would *genuinely* burst into tears and cling to your knees if you tried it."

"That's why you're one of Talesyn's," she murmured in echo.

"Keep eating, you still look a bit pale."

She shook her head. "We'll share the rest. Dessert." She'd only had five or six—there were still more than enough left in the pouch for both of them.

"We *shan't* share, because they're yours and you should eat every one of them by yourself," Corentin said loftily as she tucked the pouch away in her wet laundry where the berries wouldn't be spoiled in the heat. "But we can argue about that after dinner, I suppose."

He played for her as she got the pheasant dressed and roasting over the fire (she handed him one of its tail feathers to replace the one he'd given to Ystrac at the stone, and was very pleased with his delight, and pleased twice over to see that the arrangement of feathers in his hat was much improved again).

Supper was finished just as Ystrac's hours were turning into Idunet's, the purple and green-blue cloak of evening creeping across the sky and overtaking the pinks and reds of the sunset in the west. Between the campfire and the lantern hanging above, there was more than enough light—and more than enough protection that not even a whisper of the fear of the godwood could reach them, nor even the more practical wariness of what mundane predators might be walking in the woods.

Perhaps that was... part of Ystrac's favor. Aneth turned the thought over in her mind, frowning at it. She wouldn't be able to tell if she'd lost the wilderness-fear entirely until they left the circle of the lantern's light and protection tomorrow. She hoped she hadn't—she *loved* that fear. But... there *was* value in somehow knowing beyond a shadow of a doubt that nothing would dare to approach her camp tonight, that this circle of firelight and awen-light was truly a haven of peace, a sanctuary in the middle of the great dark wood.

The pheasant was fat enough for both of them to eat their fill of rich, tender meat. Corentin did indeed try to argue again when she brought out the pouch of blackcurrants, laid out her wet laundry in the grass to dry, and began to meticulously divide the berries into two piles on a pair of handkerchiefs she'd demanded from him.

He twanged an obstinate little song on his fancy lute—the strings were gleaming like threads of fire in the gathering dark. Even with that mulish expression on his face, her eyes kept snagging on his coat and his boots, and her heart kept swooping with the amazement of the thought that *this had happened*. This day had happened—these gifts had happened—this... friendship had happened.

She smiled helplessly down at the two handkerchiefs and their piles of berries. How splendid it was, all of this.

"Hm," said Corentin pointedly. "Magic pouch."

She looked up at him in surprise, then looked down at the two piles, at the pouch in her hand which was still half full. "So it is."

"You wouldn't be able to fit those back in if you tried." It was true—each pile of blackcurrents was now a double handful.

She grinned again and kept dividing the berries in the pouch. "No excuse for not eating them, then. I can't possibly eat all these on my own."

"Tricksy woman," he muttered, half-smiling and returning to his lute. "They'll be magic berries of some kind too, I expect. They did cure your queasiness earlier. Made you look a lot brighter and perkier. You'll have to experiment to see." He plucked out a few ringing notes that sounded like the beginning of a ballad and cast her an amused, affectionate sort of look. "Wonder if they might cure my blisters."

She sat up and somehow, through that alchemy of friendship that needs no more than a glance and a nod and a gesture to make its meaning known, Corentin understood her intent, lit up, and nodded that he was ready.

She tossed a currant to him—without missing a single note in his song, he leaned a bit to the side and caught it in his mouth. They grinned at one another. She tossed him a few more, and he caught each of them just the same, until the last one bounced off his nose. He squawked in dismay, finally fumbling a chord, and Aneth laughed and laughed until the tears ran down her face—Corentin pretended to pout, but his eyes were laughing too.

"How are your blisters?" she finally said around the last lingering gurgles of her laughter, wiping the tears from her eyes.

Corentin extended both his legs and wiggled and flexed his feet in his wonderous boots. He nodded, impressed. "You know, I do think that cured them. Congratulations, Aneth of the Woods, you have a magical pouch, full of berries that heal at least minor ailments. Perhaps they will also keep you warm in the cold, or give you energy to continue onwards even when you're tired down to your bones." He eyed the pouch. "Next question is whether that's a bottomless supply, a bigger-than-it-looks supply, or an exhaustible-but-refilling supply."

Aneth shook out another handful of blackcurrants from the pouch onto each handkerchief and set the pouch aside without looking to see how much was still in it. "Not all questions need to be answered," she said, picking up each corner of one of the handkerchiefs so she could hand it over to Corentin without spilling. "And in any case, the forest provides."

"Honor to the forest and its lord, then," Corentin said, accepting the bundle of berries. He picked up a few of them and popped them in his mouth, laying the rest carefully on the cobbles by his knee.

Aneth laid back, her head pillowed on her bag, eating the blackcurrants slowly one by one, popping each berry against the roof of her mouth with her tongue and tasting the bloom of tartness and unexpected sweetness and summer fill her senses again and again. Corentin played his lute and sang softly nearby; the campfire crackled, sending sparks dancing up into the stars above; the awen-lit lantern burned steady and unflickering like a third moon above them.

How splendid, she thought, her eyes stinging suddenly with tears. How splendid, to be here in this place, with her mouth full of summer and her ears full of music and her heart full of pride and happiness and humble gratitude. How splendid, to have a friend beside her to share equally in all of that.

She was Aneth of the Woods—oh, she did like that a great deal—and she needed no jewels or pretty dresses or coin, for she had all the wealth and beauty that she could hold right here at her fingertips, bursting with ripeness and staining her lips and tongue with sweetness.

About the Author

Alexandra Rowland is the author of *A Conspiracy Of Truths, A Choir of Lies, Some By Virtue Fall,* and *A Taste of Gold and Iron* (forthcoming August 2022 from Tor.Com Publishing), as well as a Hugo Award-nominated podcaster, all sternly supervised by their feline quality control manager. They hold a degree in world literature, mythology, and folklore from Truman State University.

Find Alexandra and more of their work at their website, and sign up for their newsletter to be notified about new releases.

Want to talk to other fans of their work? Join their fan community at their official Discord server.

Patreon | Twitter | Instagram

ALSO BY ALEXANDRA ROWLAND

THE HISTORIES OF ARTHWEND
AND THE WIDE WORLD:

A Taste of Gold and Iron (forthcoming)

<u>The Tales of the Chants:</u>
A Conspiracy of Truths
A Choir of Lies
Over All the Earth

<u>The Seven Gods Series:</u>
Some by Virtue Fall
The Lights of Ystrac's Wood

OTHER WORKS:
In The End

ALEXANDRA ROWLAND

Finding Faeries

"In Our Own Image: Radical Empathy, Trickster Gods, and the Importance of Being Irritating"